FIVE ALIEN ELVES

BY GREGORY MAGUIRE

ILLUSTRATED BY
ELAINE CLAYTON

■ HarperTrophy®
An Imprint of HarperCollins*Publishers*

Five Alien Elves
Text copyright © 1998 by Gregory Maguire
Illustrations copyright © 1998 by Elaine Clayton
HarperCollins Children's Books, a division of HarperCollins
Publishers, 1350 Avenue of the Americas,
New York, NY 10019.

Library of Congress Cataloging-in-Publication Data
Maguire, Gregory.
  Five alien elves / by Gregory Maguire ; illustrated by Elaine
Clayton.
     p.   cm.
  Summary: The town of Hamlet has a very unusual Christmas
when aliens crash land in their spaceship, escalating the competition
between rival clubs the Copycats and the Tattletales.
  ISBN 0-06-440764-0 (pbk.)
  [1. Extraterrestrial beings—Fiction.   2. Christmas—Fiction.
3. Clubs—Fiction.]   I. Clayton, Elaine, ill.   II. Title.
PZ7.M2762Fi   2000   00-20962
[Fic]—DC21   CIP
                                                                 AC

First Harper Trophy edition, 2000
Originally published by Clarion, 1998
❖
Visit us on the World Wide Web!
www.harperchildrens.com

Twinkle twinkle shooting star,
Faster than a racing car.
Up above the world so high,
Like a taxi in the sky,
Will you pick me up in case
I need a ride to outer space?

This book is for Noah and Sophie Medvedow Kazis,
and for their parents, Jill and Richard.

Contents

1

Crashing Through the Snow in a Beat-Up UFO

'Twas the night before Christmas, and you know the rest. The stockings were hung by the chimneys with care and, in one house, Superglue. The youngest kids were already in bed. Many adults were saying, "If you don't go to sleep, Santa Claus is *never* going to come!"

Something *was* coming. But it wasn't Santa Claus.

In wobbly circles, an unidentified flying object was whisking over the town of Hamlet, Vermont. The UFO was shaped like a Big Mac, only without grease dripping from the bottom. If the night hadn't been so cold, maybe more people would have been out caroling. More folks would have sighted the UFO. But the few people who looked up thought they were seeing a shooting star. A shooting star doing loop-de-loops.

Inside the UFO, an argument was in progress.

"What's the matter with you? Where'd you get

your license, the Milky Way Mall?" snorted Peppa, shaking her fingerpod at her younger brother.

"You think you can do a better job, try it," snapped Droyd. "The gravity on this planet is something fierce. I can't hold the wheel."

"You've had one glass of germ juice too many, you," said Peppa. "Get your mitts off that wheel and let me take over."

Droyd slid his oily green butt off the saddle and slithered over to the window. "It's a very strange world, Peppa," he said. "So white, and all those leafless, lifeless trees! I don't like it. I get a bad feeling. Let's alert the others. They can steer us out of this planet's gravity."

"We won't crash. I'm a great driver," said Peppa, as she twirled the steering wheel like a pro. "Now why don't you make yourself useful? Find out if this place is inhabited. Try to pick up something on the radio-wave scanner."

"You mean the Galaxy Blaster?" said Droyd. He lifted a fingerpod and pressed a switch. Static screeched at once, like fingernails on blackboards. Peppa and Droyd didn't know what fingernails were, or blackboards. But they reacted the same way anyone in the universe does. They hunched up their shoulders (or what passed for shoulders). They clenched their teeth in the back of their mouths and tightened the lids around their eyes. "Is *that* how the locals speak? I'll never learn the language," said Droyd.

"You silly thing, you already learned the language. We're speaking it right now. Our WordSearch dials teach us any local dialect we're within brain waves of."

"Listen! I've got something!" Droyd's yellow eyes throbbed out of their sockets.

Though scratchy with interference, some musical words came through. "We wish you a Merry Christmas, we wish you a Merry Christmas." Droyd looked at Peppa, not understanding. "We wish you a Merry Christmas and a Happy New Year."

"What's a Hairy Crust-mess?" said Droyd.

"You are. Blow your noses, you're dripping," said Peppa meanly. She handed her brother some paper nose wipes. But the next thing they heard made even Peppa breathe in sharply.

Now bring us a figgy pudding,
now bring us a figgy pudding.
Now bring us a figgy pudding,
and bring it right here!

"Oh, Peppa!" said Droyd. Tears formed behind his ears and dripped all the way down into his traveling socks. "It must be a message from the government. They know we're here! Five Fixipuddlings from the planet of Fixipuddle! They're calling for us! What shall we do?"

Peppa tried to look brave, but she trembled a little bit. And then the space ship started to shimmy.

Were the guards of this planet sending out crash-vibes to cause their little starship *Loiterbug* to falter? The on-line encyclopedia had said this planet was mild and somewhat backward. Peppa hadn't expected a hostile welcome!

"Droyd, I'm afraid we may be in for a bigger adventure than we expected," she said, biting her lips. "Perhaps you should go wake up Narr, Foomie, and Pimplemuss. If we're going down into captivity, we'd better all be awake and on our best behavior."

The shimmy became a shake, and the shake became a shudder. Peppa pulled up on the throttle and tried to activate the fibrillator fins, but something went wrong. "Droyd!" she screamed. "Everyone! Crash positions! Put on your safety socks! We're going down!"

2

Dasher and Dancer and Prancer and So On

A couple of miles away, a holiday party was in full swing at the Josiah Fawcett Elementary School.

The children of Miss Earth's class were dizzy with good cheer. Well, why not? It felt strange to be in the classroom at night, especially since the classroom had been transformed.

All the desks were pushed back against the wall. Hanging from the light fixtures, pine boughs glittered with white lights. Tinsel dangled along the flagpole. Holly was bunched in the pencil jar. Swags of greenery looped from the chalk tray. Even the gerbil cage sported a sprig of plastic mistletoe, which the gerbils were munching on with gusto.

Pearl Hotchkiss staggered around, blindfolded, with a red rubber ball held out in her right hand. She was trying to Pin the Red Nose on Rudolph. (Hector Yellow, the best artist in the class, had sketched a picture of a noseless reindeer on the blackboard.) Pearl almost landed the nose on the toe of Miss Earth's stocking, which hung with fifteen others on the bulletin board. All her classmates screeched with laughter, so she backed up and tried again.

Miss Earth was blowing her nose into a hankie embroidered with patterns of holly and mistletoe. She had been out sick for the last few days of school due to a bad December cold. Her students had voted to postpone their holiday party until she was well enough to join them. Since Christmas Eve was the first available moment, a classroom party was jingle-belling along for another fifteen minutes. Then parents would arrive to pick up their kids.

Salim Bannerjee wasn't used to American Christmas customs since he had recently moved to Vermont from India. He tugged at his teacher's sleeve. "Can't you read to us?" he said. "Finish that interesting story?"

"I had meant to conclude our read-aloud, Charles Dickens's *A Christmas Carol*, before our December vacation arrived," said Miss Earth, "so we could find out if Ebenezer Scrooge survives his evening with the Ghost of Christmas Yet To Come. But I was sick. And now, Salim, your classmates seem too wound up to sit still for a read-aloud session. I'm afraid it'll have to wait till the New Year."

"We all know how it ends," said Nina Bueno. "I mean, everybody grows up with *A Christmas Carol*."

"*I* don't know how it ends," said Salim sadly. "I didn't grow up with it. It's so hard to be an alien sometimes."

"I'll tell you the ending," said Nina.

"No," said Salim. "Painful though it is to wait, I'd rather hear it in the words of Mister Charles Dickens than in the slang of a fellow classmate."

"Suit yourself," said Nina. "I never thought of you as an alien before."

"*Alien* means 'a visitor from a foreign land,'" said Miss Earth. "That's all. We were all aliens at one point, even the Native Americans, if you go back far enough."

Pearl almost pinned the reindeer nose on the painting of the father of our country, George Washington. More squeals of laughter warned her away.

"To teach you about how Americans celebrate this holiday, Salim, we really should be singing carols," murmured Miss Earth, "but with this head cold, I can't possibly lead the singing." Her pupils adored Miss Earth too much to remind her that even in the pink of health she couldn't carry a tune to save her life.

"I'll turn on the Ernie Latucci show on WAAK, 99.7 FM," said Miss Earth. "Maybe there'll be a holiday sing-along airing."

Pearl was coming close to the snout of the reindeer. All her friends held their breaths. The room was still. In the silence, everyone heard the zany announcer, Ernie Latucci, broadcasting live out of the studio in nearby Crank's Corners.

"Yes, folks!" came the excited voice of Ernie Latucci. "You heard it here first! Reports just in from NORAD that an unidentified flying object has been sighted over the North Pole! It's flying below radar so we can't tell its precise destination, but an F-16 dispatched from the Hudson Bay has just broadcast a report! The UFO appears to be an airborne sleigh pulled by eight flying reindeer."

The cheery voice of Ernie Latucci gave a laugh. "Stay tuned to WAAK, the Voice of Vermont! We'll bring you the update on what appears to be a Santa sighting! On Dasher, on Dancer, on Prancer, on Vixen; on Lucy, on Ricky, on Ethel, and so on! Don't go away! Now, for you folks heading home on the interstate, here's something you can sing along to! On the count of three! One, two, three!"

A brass band launched into the introduction of "We Wish You a Merry Christmas." Miss Earth's mother, Grandma Earth, who was helping out with the refreshments, waved an eggnog ladle as a baton. Most of the children began to sing.

We wish you a Merry Christmas,
we wish you a Merry Christmas.
We wish you a Merry Christmas,
and a Happy New Year!
Good tidings we bring to you and your kin.
Good tidings for Christmas and a Happy New Year!

They all thought that was the end of the song, but the rollicking chorus on the radio continued with another verse.

> *Now bring us a figgy pudding,*
> *now bring us a figgy pudding.*
> *Now bring us a figgy pudding,*
> *and bring it right here!*

Because Grandma Earth was a baker, she knew what a figgy pudding was. It was something like a fruitcake: rich and dark and dense and sweet. But it wasn't very popular, at least not in America. Maybe back in England, where this song had first come from—but not in Vermont. To Americans, a figgy pudding was a kind of alien dessert.

"Big finish!" cried Grandma Earth. She began to do the cha-cha around the eggnog, which was set on the audio-visual cart. Her daughter grabbed onto her waist, and the students joined on next, one by one. Soon they were all shaking their hips and doing the Christmas conga to the last chorus.

> *We wish you a Merry Christmas,*
> *we wish you a Merry Christmas.*
> *We wish you a Merry Christmas*
> *and a Happy New Year!*

Pearl punched the red nose on the correct spot, where it stuck, thanks to the rolled-up masking tape applied to one side of the ball. Then she tore off her blindfold.

"Yes! I won!" she exclaimed, just as the door flew open. In waddled a big-bellied figure in a red flannel suit and a red cap with a white cotton pom-pom on the tip. His snowy beard looked like the stuffing of a pillow.

"Santa Claus," said Fawn Petros, who was old enough not to believe in Santa anymore, but still wondered. She blinked shyly at him.

"Ho ho ho," said Santa Claus in a familiar voice.

"It's Mayor Grass!" shrieked the other students. Fawn began to pout.

Mayor Timothy Grass, a goodhearted soul, sat himself down in Miss Earth's reading rocker. "I think you're all too big to sit on my lap," he said in a deep voice, like Darth Vader speaking through a paper towel tube. "But please, dear children, tell me what you want for Christmas."

Thekla Mustard was Empress of a club called the Tattletales. Except for Pearl Hotchkiss, all the girls in the class belonged to the club. Thekla was used to speaking up first, and speak up first she did.

"I want peace on Earth, good will to men, women, and children," said Thekla, clearly announcing every virtuous syllable.

"And dogs," said Lois Kennedy the Third, whose dog Reebok, by special permission, had joined the holiday party. Reebok thumped his tail on the floor, but declined to make further comment.

Instead he chewed happily on the sock Lois had hung up as her stocking. It had been so easy to nip down from the bulletin board, and was so much fun to rip apart.

"Peace to all men, women, children, and dogs of every race, creed, color, and degree of marvelousness," said Thekla. "Peace on Earth. That's all I ask."

Sammy Grubb rolled his eyes. He was the Chief of the Copycats club, which counted all the boys in the classroom as its members. He wasn't to be outdone by his rival, Thekla Mustard. "For Christmas, I want Bigfoot the Snow Monster to come out of the woods and eat up Thekla Mustard," he said, "and *then* peace on Earth might be a distant possibility."

All the boys laughed. Thekla turned pink. Partly she was irked at the insult, and partly she was pleased at the publicity.

Miss Earth sneezed seven times in a row. "What do you want for Christmas, Miss Earth?" said Mayor Santa Claus Grass.

"You mean besides a cure for the common cold? Well, peace on Earth may be a bit much to hope for," said Miss Earth, "so I'd settle for peace in Miss Earth's classroom. I wish the Tattletales and the Copycats would stop trying to outdo each other at every step. . . . You children should all take a lesson from Pearl Hotchkiss, who doesn't belong to either club and is perfectly happy being friends with everyone. Pearl, what do you wish for?"

It was Pearl's turn to blush. What she really wanted was for Sammy Grubb to take a shine to her. But she would rather be kidnapped by space aliens than admit such a thing aloud. So she said, "I hope I get Kung Fu Barbie."

"I want a paint box with a hundred and forty-four colors," said Hector Yellow.

"I want a glow-in-the-dark rosary," said Anna Maria Mastrangelo.

"We don't do Christmas," said Moshe Cohn, "but for the last night of Hanukkah I want a chemistry set for inventing useful potions."

"Gotcha," said Mayor Santa Claus Grass. "I like useful potions myself." He took a swig of eggnog.

"I want my own portable hair dryer," said Carly Garfunkel, swishing her hair showily.

"I want a ten-speed bike," said Forest Eugene Mopp, "a green one."

"We celebrate Kwaanza," said Sharday Wren. "And for Kwaanza I want new ballet slippers. My old ones smell."

"I want the new CD by Modest Well-Bred Youths," said Stan Tomaski, "the one with the hit single called 'Floss Often and Respect Your Elders.'"

"I want a penguin costume," said Fawn Petros. Everyone looked at her. "My father is a penguin scientist," she explained, kind of.

"I want a pink sequined sweater with matching pink sequined socks," said Nina Bueno.

"I want a new outfit, too," said Lois Kennedy the Third, but she didn't specify what sort of outfit she wanted.

Everyone looked at Salim Bannerjee, who was the only one left. "What do you want for Christmas?" asked Mayor Timothy Santa Claus Grass.

"We're not Christian," said Salim, a bit confused. "I'm half Muslim and half Hindu. Do I still get what I want?"

"Sometimes," said Sammy Grubb.

"If you're *good* enough," said Thekla Mustard, primping to beat the band.

"If Santa Claus hears you," whispered Fawn Petros hopefully.

"Then," said Salim, "we're having such a fun time tonight, I want the clock to turn back an hour right now so we can start this party all over again! We can be the Ghosts of Christmas Past—I mean, an hour past! Then Miss Earth will have time to finish reading *A Christmas Carol* to us!" He ran and got the book off her desk.

Everyone turned and looked at the clock. It didn't roll back an hour.

"Time rarely shifts its chronic pattern just because you request it," explained Thekla Mustard. "Can you think of something a little less ridiculous?"

"I want a mint sweetie?" said Salim. Fawn handed him one.

"Oh, I see," he said. "This is a great game."

"Of course, there isn't really any such thing as Santa Claus," began Sammy Grubb.

"Oh, yeah?" said Thekla Mustard hotly. "Well, there isn't any such thing as Bigfoot either, for your information—"

But before the argument could heat up, Miss Earth said, "Children, children. A holiday party is a time for peace and good will. Besides, your parents are due any minute. Shall we look out the window and check if anyone's arrived and waiting?"

Grumbling good-naturedly, the children hurried to the window to see if any cars had pulled into the parking lot yet. So they all witnessed the brightness streaking across the sky.

"Look, a shooting star!" cried Miss Earth. "Make a wish!"

Suddenly Reebok leaped to his feet and began to bark furiously. "What is it, boy?" said Lois. "Something spook you? I wish you could talk. That's my wish on the shooting star!"

"Ruff," said Reebok, as obligingly as he could.

"I mean in English," said Lois. "I think I know what you mean to say, but sometimes I can't tell, and it's kind of—"

"Ruff," said Reebok.

"Exactly," said Lois.

The shooting star, or whatever it was, disappeared, but it left a scar of ice-blue vapor in the dusk.

3

You Better Watch Out, You Better Not Cry

Old Man Fingerpie was in Florida with his wife, Flossie Fingerpie. He and Flossie were busy mixing up some holiday martinis for their winter friends when the spaceship from the planet of Fixipuddle crash-landed next to their barn in Hamlet, Vermont. The barn was empty of living things except mice in the straw and owls in the eaves. At the sound of the crash the mice burrowed deeper into their nests. The owls blinked once or twice at each other as if to say *How very peculiar.*

Inside the starship *Loiterbug,* the Fixipuddlings were checking themselves to see if they were still alive.

"My baby tooth broke off," said Droyd. "It was my last one." He started to cry. "Now the tooth alien will never come and put a pickle or a lime under my pillow."

Peppa crawled out from under the table. "You

dolt, tooth aliens give nickels or dimes, not pickles or limes. Your WordSearch dial has been jostled in the crash. Better reset it."

"A tooth is a tooth," said Droyd. He put his tooth in his belly pouch. It was a *baby* baby tooth—only eight inches long. "I guess I should go check on the others."

The door was flung open before he could get there.

"What—have—you—done—*now!*" The voice was cold and slow, like the knelling of a deep-throated gong.

"Peppa did it," said Droyd.

"Droyd did it," said Peppa at the same time.

Their leader, Pimplemuss, stood quivering in all her awful glory. She was nine feet tall and downy white, shaped something like a huge goose on three legs. A row of eyes ran from her forehead to her belly pouch. She wore her sleeping socks, and she carried an empty cup in her tentacle. A yellow stain across her chest showed what had happened to the hot corn tea.

"I leave you alone for half a year, and look what you get into!" snapped Pimplemuss. "I was just settling down to read myself a little inspirational verse and take a nap. I ought to boot you right out into the nether depths of space!"

"Can't do that now," said Droyd in a small voice. "Look."

With her free tentacle, Pimplemuss rubbed her

eyes, one after the other. One after the other they blinked. She looked out the window with all six eyes. "Horrible heavens, what is that?" she roared.

Droyd cowered behind his big sister.

"It's a world," said Peppa. "We're sorry, Pimplemuss. We made a boo-boo."

"Do you mean to tell me we've made *landfall*? And I in my sleeping socks?" In rage, Pimplemuss opened up her mouth, which was not a pretty sight. It looked like half-chewed pizza. "You two have a lot to answer for! Do you have any idea where we are?"

"We were just cruising around, Pimplemuss," said Peppa. She tried to be brave. "We were bored. There's never anything for us to do."

"Narr!" shouted Pimplemuss. "Foomie! Get out here! Look what these twerps have done!"

She swept the smaller Fixipuddlings aside with one mighty tentacle and sent her cup crashing against the door. "*Narr!*" she shouted again. "We're castaways on a deserted planet!"

Narr appeared. He looked like Pimplemuss, only less so. Less energetic, less tall, less angry. Narr was old and didn't talk anymore. Opinions took so much energy. However, he had one opinion: He didn't like Pimplemuss when she was in this mood.

"What is this place? It looks like acres of salt out there, scattered over the landscape!" said Pimplemuss. "Narr, how can a world be covered with salt?"

Narr shrugged his hips. He pulled on his thin paper socks, which drooped. He didn't have any idea.

"Foomie?" said Pimplemuss. Her voice was getting lower. Droyd laced his fingerpods through his big sister's and squeezed. Boy, they were in *really big trouble* this time.

Narr moved aside. Foomie stepped delicately in. With shorter legs than Pimplemuss, Foomie looked more like a mutant chicken than a giant goose. Foomie was a guest on this flight and had not expected to have to voice an opinion. Technically Foomie was both male and female, but in the language they were struggling to master, Foomie was most easily identified, simply, as Foomie.

Foomie cleared Foomie's throat. "Oh, have the little ones done something naughty?"

"I'll say naughty, I'll say nasty, I'll say FOUR HUNDRED YEARS STANDING IN THE CORNER NAUGHTY," shouted Pimplemuss.

"Well, let's not get our tentacles in a knot, shall we?" said Foomie. "I'm sure they're very sorry. Aren't you, dears?" Foomie blinked three eyelids at a time.

"We didn't *mean* to crash the starship," said Droyd.

"We'll help you fix it," said Peppa.

"If we can even get it fixed," said Pimplemuss. "I have a good mind to leave you here for a thousand years to think over how bad you've been. Do you hear me?"

The young Fixipuddlings hadn't gone through adolescence yet. They still looked more like greasy baby squid than like three-legged giant fowl. Their oil ran down their flanks like beads of sweat. They nodded at Pimplemuss's threat. Even Narr and Foomie nodded, though they hadn't done anything wrong. When Pimplemuss was in a bad mood, the best thing was to be agreeable.

"Okay, we better learn about this desolate slag heap of a planet," said Pimplemuss. "I assume our power supply is still working. Can you get a scan going on the scan-o-matic?"

Narr hobbled over to a machine that looked like a cross between a microwave oven and a parlor organ. He fussed over the dials and keys.

"Pimplemuss," said Peppa, "there's something we should tell you."

Pimplemuss paid no attention. "Foomie, if you'd be so kind," she said, "dial the emergency number for the Astrospace Autovehicle Association. Tell them I'm on a mission to earn a merit badge and have gotten sidetracked somewhere. They'll send out a towship if you sound desperate enough."

"I'll positively bleat," said Foomie, and went to the dial pad.

"This is important," said Peppa nervously.

"Peppa's right," said Droyd. "Listen to her."

"What are you numskulls on about now?" shouted

Pimplemuss. "Don't you think you've made enough of a mess—"

She was interrupted by the scan-o-matic, which announced with a shriek that it was working. Narr ran to the other side of the cabin and hid behind a bank of computers. Foomie got the emergency number all wrong and had to hang up. Pimplemuss looked as if she had swallowed a sandwich made out of carpet tacks. They all swiveled to look at the screen of the scan-o-matic.

"Oh, my socks and starships," murmured Pimplemuss. "This is worse than I thought. This planet has *creatures* on it!"

"And what ugly cusses they are," said Foomie, fluffing Foomie's white feathers in distaste.

"That's what I was trying to tell you," muttered Droyd mournfully.

"Look!" said Pimplemuss, but she didn't need to. They all *were* looking.

20

4

The Dictator of the World

The scan-o-matic was a smart device. It could supply a written report on the atmosphere, geology, and real estate value of whatever planet happened to be nearest. But now it was showing something new. Something it had never shown before. It was broadcasting a picture, a moving picture.

"It's creepy," murmured Foomie. "It's like something is dripping on the screen. It keeps changing shape as you watch. I don't like it at all."

The Fixipuddlings stared, fascinated. On the screen they could see a kind of factory. Dozens of little workers in red caps and green suspenders rushed around looking frantic. They were making some kind of industrial product. There were wooden soldiers with guns. There were glassy-eyed baby dolls. There were stuffed bears. The workers packed these products into boxes.

"That looks like slave labor to me," hissed Pimplemuss. "Look how hard those little guys are working! And what are those little statues of soldiers and babies and bears *used* for?"

As they watched the screen, they saw a door fling open.

There stood a creature with a whole lot of white fur on his face and chin. He was dressed entirely in red, complete with a red hat trimmed with a dollop of more white fur. He was clearly the boss. The little workers came running to his side, dragging heavy sacks full of boxes. The boss led them to a sled standing outside the door. Harnessed to the sled were some sort of long-legged poodles, including one with a bright red nose. The red-clad creature jumped onto the front of the sled, cracked his whip, and cried, "Ho ho ho!"

"Ho ho who?" said Pimplemuss. "Who *is* this?"

The poodle-like animals strained at the reins, and the sled began to move. It rose in the air like some old-fashioned space vehicle. The old driver left the factory and the little slaves behind, and laughed a long series of ho ho ho's.

After a while the sled landed on the roof of a building. The red-clad creature got out of the sled, hoisting one of the huge sacks onto his back. He winked in a cunning fashion and climbed into a chimney.

"He's breaking into that house!" cried Droyd.

Next they saw the red old thing crawling out of

the fireplace, right inside the house. He tiptoed into a bedroom where some strange little beings lay sleeping with smiles on their faces.

"Oh, this is dreadful! I could never stand horror stories! I can't watch!" cried Peppa, and flung her fingerpods over her face. But she peered out between them.

The creature in the red suit didn't touch the sleeping mites. Instead he returned to the common room, where he found a modest plate of food and a glass of white liquid. He ate every last morsel and drank the glass dry.

"That greedy guzzle-gut! He's sucking down what little food they have!" said Droyd.

Then the creature took from his sack some of the boxes containing the bears, the babies, the soldiers. Only you couldn't tell which was which, because the boxes were now wrapped in colored paper. He put the boxes underneath a house plant decorated with baubles.

"The villain!" seethed Pimplemuss. "He's leaving some sort of trap for those innocent creatures! Those bears and soldiers and babies must be enemy agents! Or spies! Domestic spies! Look how he's disguised them with bright paper and ribbons! We must save these people! Fate has brought us here!"

"Pimplemuss, get ahold of those motherly instincts," said Foomie in a reasonable voice. "Let's not run amuck here. You're itching for a planet to save so you can earn your merit badge, I know. But let's watch awhile longer and see what happens next."

"That old fiend must be the dictator of this world," said Pimplemuss. "He must be stopped!"

"Oh, you haven't had your nap, I see," said Foomie.

"Don't be snarky," said Pimplemuss. Foomie looked apologetic. But Foomie kept watching the scan-o-matic.

The old red-clad creature went flying away, laughing his fiendish signature cackle of "Ho ho ho!" It was the most dreadful thing any of them had ever witnessed. Peppa and Droyd clutched each other and whimpered. Narr's lower lip wobbled and he bit it.

Then the scene changed. An old woman looked ill and crabby. She stretched her limbs. A pattern of glowing lights illuminated her back muscles. She opened a bottle of tablets and jostled a couple into her hand.

"Don't eat them!" shouted Pimplemuss. "That monster must have left them for you when he snuck into your home!" But it was too late.

The old woman chewed. She swallowed. She smiled instantly and raised her arms over her head as if surrendering.

"Look, it *was* lethal," said Pimplemuss. "Now that woman is acting like an idiot." And she was. She was jumping around with a racket, hitting a shuttlecock back and forth with an equally athletic man. The glowing patterns in her limbs were gone.

"What's she doing? It looks as if it wouldn't be too boring," murmured Droyd to Peppa.

"What's the point?" said Pimplemuss, overhearing. "Why doesn't she just catch the thing and throw it out, instead of batting it back and forth like that?"

Words flashed across the screen. "For fast relief of muscular pain, take Numb-All."

"I don't know what Numb-All means," said Droyd, "even with my WordSearch dial set to *local*. The nearest I can get is *nimble*, which means 'spry and sprightly.'"

"Spry and sprightly and brain-dead, that's what Numb-All means," said Pimplemuss. "That must be how the villain controls the masses."

The picture changed again. Now the sled and the poodles were flinging themselves across a midnight sky. The sack was empty. His work done, the old monster landed his sleigh in a snowy field outside the factory.

"It's his Fortress of Fear," said Pimplemuss. "I've seen those before on other planets. Scary."

A horde of little workers came rushing to cower before the mighty giant. They unhitched the poodles and pulled the sled into a shed. "Look at those poor slaves," said Droyd. "They have to do all the work!"

After that, the little slaves helped the old man into his house. Pine boughs and tinsel and little white lights were everywhere. There was a sound of gluey-sweet singing in the background.

"I believe I'm going to be ill," said Foomie. "If you'll excuse me." Foomie hurried to the Room for Private Moments.

Just then the picture stopped. A wave of lines went back and forth across the scan-o-matic and the screen went dead.

"Well, the scan-o-matic's bit the dust," said Pimplemuss. "But we must pull ourselves together and do what needs to be done. We'd better disguise ourselves, though. What did you say this planet was called?"

"I didn't actually say," said Foomie, who had come back from Foomie's private moment. "We seem to be outside the range of any tow services. But the recording on the AAA line identified this backwater puddlestone as Earth."

"Then," said Pimplemuss, straightening up to her full nine feet, "we had better go liberate the Earthlings from the clutches of that fiend."

"Do you think it's any of our business, really?" murmured Foomie.

"Are you shirking your intergalactic duty to your fellow creature-beings?" hissed Pimplemuss.

"Not at all," said Foomie quickly.

"Besides," said Peppa eagerly, "we heard them calling us for help! 'Now bring us a Fixipuddling,' they sang! They were crying out to be rescued from this monster."

26

Pimplemuss said, "You may be right. Maybe fate has brought us here. Maybe this is my chance to do a good deed and win my merit badge. Maybe I will yet thank you, Droyd and Peppa, for your sloppy driving. Everyone, put on your warmest socks. We're going out."

Foomie said, "Pimplemuss, you and your enthusiasms . . ." Foomie looked doubtful. Narr put a trash basket over his head and pretended to take a nap. But Pimplemuss looked brave and eager as she worked the handles of the outer door.

5

How the Copycats and Tattletales Came to Be

The Christmas party was over. Most of the parents had come to pick up their children, but a couple of kids were walking home through the snow. Lois Kennedy the Third and her dog Reebok fell in alongside Sammy Grubb and Salim Bannerjee.

"How did you get to become Chief of the Copycats?" said Salim to Sammy.

"It was way back in kindergarten," said Sammy Grubb. "It was partly because of Thekla Mustard. One day during naptime, Thekla Mustard started humming the Brahms Lullaby. Ms. Frazzle, the kindergarten teacher, told her to pipe down. But Thekla got all the girls except Pearl to hum along with her, which drove us boys crazy. We started humming 'Frère Jacques' to get even. Thekla raised her hand to complain about our copying her idea of musical comfort at naptime. She called us boys copycats, and we called her and her friends tattletales. And that's how it all started."

"Fascinating," said Salim. "America is truly the land of possibility. But how did you get elected Chief?"

"For a while we just called each other copycats and tattletales," said Sammy Grubb. "But then the holiday season rolled around and we had a grab bag. Ms. Frazzle suggested all our homemade presents be hats we could wear at wild rumpus time. I think this was because she wanted an excuse to wear noise-blocking earmuffs in the classroom."

"Oh, I sort of remember this," said Lois. What she remembered more vividly, however, was her very first kindergarten show and tell. Lois had set out to make friends and influence people by displaying a little plastic bag full of her toenail clippings. Everyone was impressed until Thekla announced that she was going to show her superior brains by reciting eight lines from Hamlet's famous speech, "To be or not to be? That is the question." Lois had felt overshadowed by Thekla. Then, and ever after.

Sammy went on. "Well, when I stuck my hand in the grab bag, I pulled out a Native American headdress. It was made of cardboard, and crow's feathers were glued to it. I called myself the Chief, and it stuck. I was Chief of the Copycats."

"Unhappy memories," said Lois. "Thekla got a paper crown from Burger King. She crowned herself Empress of the Tattletales, and has been so ever since. She always wins, six votes to one. I'm the only one who ever votes for me."

"I know what you would like for Christmas," said Sammy Grubb. "You want to be elected Empress of the Tattletales. You're fed up with Thekla Mustard."

"Well, she does remind us that she is our lawful ruler," said Lois grimly, "but sometimes I say she's our *awful* ruler."

"What did you get in that grab bag, Lois?" asked Salim.

"A headband with two sproingy antennae sticking out," said Lois. "It was supposed to be a space alien hat. I traded it for a cupcake. If I couldn't be Empress, I sure didn't want to be an alien."

"I'm an alien," said Salim. "But I don't think wearing a hat like that would help me fit into the American way of life."

"You'd be surprised," said Sammy.

"And why didn't Pearl join the Tattletales?" said Salim.

"She just didn't want to," said Lois. "It's not as if she's against girls or anything. She's just independent."

Sammy said, "Oh, I just remembered something. Do either of you happen to have a dollar I could borrow?"

Salim and Lois both dug in their pockets to hunt for change.

"Why?" said Salim.

"I saw something in the Grand Union this afternoon when I was picking up candy canes for our party, but I didn't have enough money to buy it."

"What?" said Lois.

"Oh, just something I want," said Sammy. "I already have a quarter."

Lois dug out three quarters from the tip of her mitten and handed them over. Salim contributed five nickels, twelve pennies, a dime, and a mint sweetie.

"Thanks," said Sammy. "I'm only short three cents. Maybe the store will spring for it in the spirit of holiday giving. I hope you both get your Christmas wishes. And happy new year to you, too, Reebok."

The three friends parted. Salim headed across the edge of the village green. Lois turned up Squished Toad Road to her home, Reebok trotting along beside her. Supplied with cash, Sammy backtracked toward the Grand Union supermarket. He hoped that it would still be open. He wanted to buy a copy of a newspaper that proved the existence of Bigfoot. His secret wish on the shooting star had been for Bigfoot to show up and terrorize the town. Just a manageable, agreeable amount of terror.

Sammy didn't know if there really was such a creature as Bigfoot. He didn't know if it might be passing through the Green Mountains of Vermont. But Christmas is a time of hope.

6

Elves Themselves

At the open door of the starship *Loiterbug,* a blast of cold air hit the faces of the five Fixipuddlings. They peered out and sniffed and wiggled their earshells.

"What a weird planet," said Peppa. "All this white stuff."

"They call it snow," said Pimplemuss. "Someone ought to clear it up."

"Should one of us stay behind and guard the starship?" asked Foomie. "I could volunteer to give this expedition a miss."

"We must stick together," said Pimplemuss. "That's an order, Foomie. Don't be—in the language of this part of the galaxy—a fraidy cat. Besides, I think the starship is too broken for anyone to fly it."

Pimplemuss stepped out into the new world first. Droyd and Peppa, standing close together, each put a fingerpod down to feel the nerve-curdling snow. Foomie slipped back inside the starship for a minute, but soon reappeared, dressed in three sets of paper socks, one inside the other. "My tender feet are always cold," said Foomie. Narr followed, closing the door behind him.

"The air is breathable," said Pimplemuss.

"The sky is purple and black," said Droyd.

"The snow moves under your tentacles in a disgusting way," said Peppa.

"I smell something burning," said Foomie. "Carbon-based life forms of the tree variety?"

Narr kept five of his six eyes closed, and blinked the sixth eye a lot. Narr didn't want to see any more than he had to.

"What'll we do if we meet that fat old red-dressed man?" said Peppa.

"I'll punch his lights out!" said Droyd.

"You'll do nothing of the sort," said Pimplemuss. "I'm the commander in chief. I'll take charge."

"You'd better take charge right away," said Foomie, "for I do believe someone or something is coming!"

The five aliens paused in their tracks. They shivered, partly because their feet and tentacles were always cold, and partly because they were afraid.

An Earthling on four legs came ambling along the road, his tail high in the air, wagging back and forth. He had a pinkish tongue sticking out in a droll way, and he was covered with a close-cut brown and white fringe.

"Halt! I bring greetings from the planet of Fixipuddle!" said Pimplemuss, drawing herself up tall and trying to keep any two of her six eyes from crossing.

The creature looked at Pimplemuss. He sniffed a bit. He sniffed a bit more and looked puzzled. But he didn't speak.

"Gracious, what's wrong, do I smell?" said Pimplemuss, mortified. "I washed only a month ago."

The creature opened his mouth and rapped a series of edgy retorts at Pimplemuss.

"I'm afraid I don't understand," said Pimplemuss politely. She fiddled with her WordSearch dial. "Accents can be so misleading. . . . Could you repeat yourself?"

The creature obliged, yapping again.

"What is it, Reebok?" called a voice from around a bend in the road. "I hope you haven't treed a raccoon or something. Come here."

"*That* I understood," said Pimplemuss. "It's in the language the WordSearch dials are teaching us. We must prepare to meet the locals. Everyone, spit spot, look your best!"

But as Droyd straightened his spines and smiled, his oily tentacles slipped on a patch of ice. His green bottom kerplunked into a drift of snow and he let out a wail.

34

The four-legged creature howled, and yipped, and backed up, looking nervous.

"What is it, boy?" said the voice, coming nearer.

Pimplemuss said uneasily, "The Earthling seems alarmed. Maybe he is shocked at our beauty. He isn't much to look at himself, is he? We don't want to intimidate the ugly residents of Earth with our physical glory. Perhaps we should rethink our plan."

"Come here, Reebok! It's all right. Here, boy!" said the voice.

The thing called Reebok whined again. Then he growled. The Fixipuddlings didn't like the growling part.

"I don't think we can risk an intergalactic crisis over being too beautiful to behold," said Pimplemuss. Reebok growled again, lower in his throat, and showed some teeth.

"Double quick, back to the starship!" said Pimplemuss.

Old stiff-limbed Narr had just made it through the doorway, and the door had just shut, when the other Earthling came around the bend of the road and into view. The Fixipuddlings stared at her through the window.

It was one of the young ones. Like the sleeping creatures they saw broadcast on the screen. A female.

The creature called Reebok was cavorting all around her, leaping up and down like a crazy

35

thing. "What's the matter, boy? Old Man Fingerpie's place give you the creeps? Don't worry, nothing around here but old hoot owls and the occasional deer. You're just excitable because it's Christmas Eve and you're out late. Yes, yes, that party was lots of fun. But the quicker we get to sleep, the quicker it'll be tomorrow."

The female was dressed in a red parka with a blue knitted ski cap and blue mittens. She had dark hair, cut shoulder length, and her boots were red plastic. "Do you think Santa Claus knows where Reebok lives? Do you think he will come in his sleigh tonight and find Lois Kennedy the Third? Whaddya say?"

The female passed out of view. She never even saw the starship *Loiterbug.*

"We must disguise ourselves," said Pimplemuss, "and follow that girl. We can snoop around and learn more about this fat old evil fellow and how to overthrow him. Yes, a makeover," decided Pimplemuss. "Quick! Everyone, into the particle shower."

The Fixipuddlings hustled themselves into the particle shower stall. It was crowded, but they were in a hurry. They didn't want to lose this precious lead. "Close your eyes," said Pimplemuss, "and empty your minds of all thought."

"It's not hard after centuries in space," mumbled Peppa. "There isn't anything out there to fill our minds up *with.*"

"Shush," snapped Pimplemuss. "We don't have all evening."

She turned the knob and adjusted the nozzle. She attached an electric mesh cap to her head. "This hairnet will pick up my brainwaves, so I have to think of a perfect disguise. Maybe those little worker creatures. I think the right word is *elves.* It's a *perfect* disguise, at least to start out with." The electric hairnet began to glow orange, like the element in a toaster. "Everyone ready? Here goes."

She pressed the on button. The five explorers from Fixipuddle looked at one another in interest and fear as, one by one, they began to dissolve in the air. Droyd and Peppa's green fingerpods and oily tentacles. Narr's nervous, bloodshot eyes. Foomie's elegant feather-do. The nine-foot Pimplemuss with her vertical row of glaring eyes.

In their place appeared five elves.

Droyd wore shorts and a little jacket.

Peppa had a green and red bow in her hair and a flouncy skirt shaped like a lampshade.

Narr was a vaporish elf with a long beard that trailed almost to the floor. He sported suspenders with a design of holly and berries on them. His nervous beard fluttered around the edges.

Pimplemuss was a stout female elf, about three feet tall. She wore a white smock with a yellow stain across the front. Her braided hair was corn silk yellow and so were her large teeth.

Foomie said, "Well, not so bad. What do you

think?" Foomie was dressed in red and green plaid trousers with a matching vest and a cap with a feather in it. But Foomie's hair was a bit wild; it covered most of Foomie's face.

"We have no time to do it over," said Pimplemuss, looking at her hands. "Is this what hands are? How awkward. Can everyone manage on two legs? I know we should have practiced this makeover stuff, but we need to save the juice to turn ourselves back."

"Look, I even have a red and green handkerchief," said Foomie. "Talk about coordinated outfits! Pimplemuss, you think of everything."

"Everyone's got their WordSearch dial still attached? Good. We are going to run," said Pimplemuss. "All right, crew. On the count of four!"

"I miss my tentacles," said Peppa, sniffling.

"One! Three! Two! Whatever!" shouted Pimplemuss. "Move! Move! Move!"

The five alien elves departed the starship *Loiterbug* and hit the road at a trot. The girl had disappeared, but they could still hear Reebok howling ahead. That was a good sign. Pimplemuss led the way, her stout little knees pumping up and down. The five Fixipuddlings were surprised to find that elf legs, though uglier than most limbs they'd ever seen in the galaxy, could run pretty quickly.

7

Deck the Halls with Poison Ivy

Lois Kennedy the Third kicked off her boots and threw them under the back stairs. Reebok shook the snow off his fur. He ran to his bowl, hoping against hope to find something he had forgotten to eat at dinner. From the dining room came the sound of Christmas music on the radio.

"I'm home," yelled Lois.

"Shhh," said her mom. "Your little brother is asleep. How was the party?"

"Okay. Is that Santa Claus movie still on?"

"It finished already. It's getting late. Now go brush your teeth and get in your pajamas, and you'll be asleep before you know it."

"I sure hope Santa brings me what I want," said Lois.

"What is that?" said her mom.

"Haven't I mentioned it before? A double-breasted trench coat with loops on the belt for carrying things. With big pockets, and a collar that you can flip up against the rain. I wouldn't mind a pair of dark glasses and a man's fedora, either."

Lois's dad threw another log in the cast-iron stove. "Why ever do you want a getup like that?" he said.

"Because the club I belong to is called the Tattletales," said Lois patiently. "What does it really mean to be a tattletale but to be a spy? You have to know things before you can tattle. Spies find things out. But it's not enough to be just a good spy. I want to be the Empress. And every time we have a vote for leader, Thekla Mustard wins."

"I don't understand how a spy outfit would make you Empress of the Tattletales," said Lois's mom. "Put your finger there while I tie this ribbon. Press hard. That's good."

"You see," said Lois, "Thekla rules by her brains. And why not? That's all she has."

"Lois!" said her mother. "Thekla is a very good-looking girl."

"Mom," said Lois, "if you ran into Thekla Mustard in a dark alley, you'd take her for a space alien having a bad hair day."

"That's out-and-out unkind, and I don't approve of talk like that, missy," said her mother. "Why are you so down on Thekla?"

"Thekla has been my chief rival for power since kindergarten," said Lois grimly. "Who got to hold the stop sign when Mayor Grass came to talk to us about traffic safety? Thekla Mustard. Who won first prize in the joke-a-thon to raise money for a new playground? Thekla Mustard. And ever since the Tattletales were formed, Thekla has been elected Empress about a thousand times in a row."

"Being Empress isn't everything in life," mused Mr. Kennedy. "Though I admit, Empress Lois has a nice ring to it."

"A trench coat will improve my public profile," said Lois Kennedy the Third. "A new vote will be demanded by the other Tattletales. I'll accept the nomination with grace and modesty. And then I'll run roughshod over Thekla Mustard, and power will be mine at last! Ha ha ha ha ha ha ha!" She threw back her head and laughed in a power-hungry way. She was only partly kidding.

Reebok put his paws over his eyes and sunk his chin into his bowl and licked for crumbs.

"What a charming Christmas thought," said Mrs. Kennedy. "Charity and warmth to all. Well, I knew we were raising a peppery individual, but I didn't know what a good job we'd done."

Lois sang, "Deck the halls with poison ivy, Fa la la la la, la la la la. Why should Thekla be alive-y? Fa la la la la, la la la la."

"Lois," said her dad, "I wouldn't go *that* far. Those are pretty nervy things to say on Christmas Eve. Santa Claus is going to be checking his list to see who's been naughty or nice. He has spies everywhere. Don't forget. You better behave and be nice."

"Nice schmice," said Lois. "Santa Claus isn't going to be fooled by a little last-minute goody two-shoes shtick. Besides, I can't believe you still go

41

through this corny Santa Claus shtick with me." Nevertheless, she looked a tad unsure.

"He sees you when you're sleeping, he knows when you're awake. So go to bed," said her mom, and gave her a kiss.

Reebok put his nose in the air and sniffed. Then he started to bark. "What is it, boy?" said Mr. Kennedy. "You get a whiff of some strange reindeer on the roof?"

"Reebok's been acting weird tonight," said Lois. "I wonder why." She kissed her dad and mounted the stairs to her room, muttering, "If I get that snazzy spy outfit put together, just watch me climb to the top!"

"Keep your voice down, dear," said her mom. "Your brother, remember."

"What a character we've brought into the world," said Mr. Kennedy in a low voice, grinning at his wife.

✳

The five alien elves were on the side porch, peering in through the windows. They were watching Mr. and Mrs. Kennedy sip some eggnog. The elves were confused. When Reebok started to howl, they scurried back behind the garage, where they cleared the snow off a picnic table and sat down cross-legged to discuss what they heard.

"What was all that fa la la la stuff?" said Droyd. "Was that Earthling crying?"

"I think it was a lullaby," said Pimplemuss.

"It's a strange world," said Peppa. "It makes me

feel weird. I wish we were back in outer space. It's a lot safer there."

"But we've learned a little bit," said Pimplemuss. "We should take it a step at a time. What can we deduce about Earth from what we just heard?"

"I think that noisy four-legged thing is a guardian from another planet," said Peppa. "It doesn't look much like an Earthling."

Pimplemuss said witheringly, "In our natural state, Peppa, you and I don't look much alike, and yet we're both the same species—just different ages. And besides, species *do* differ from one another."

"Peppa might be right about him being a guardian," said Foomie. "Did you notice how he howled when he saw us looking in the window?"

Pimplemuss ran her hands along her braids. Then she ran her tongue over her yellow-white teeth. "Well, I'll grant you that," she said. "Good for you, Peppa."

Peppa smirked a bit in Droyd's direction. Droyd found a new use for his new tongue. He stuck it out at her.

"Did anyone notice anything else?" said Pimplemuss.

Peppa said, "We found out that the awful dictator is making a list and checking it twice. He knows when everybody's sleeping or waking. He must have spies everywhere."

"What a scary name. Santa Claws!" Droyd shaped his hands to look like scary claws about to rip someone's face off.

"We found out that the girl's name is Lois," said Peppa. "She wants to be Empress of the Tattletales, whatever that is."

"I know how *that* feels," said Pimplemuss grimly. "I want to be elected Serene Queen of Fixipuddle. Did I ever mention this before?"

"Yes," they answered, except Narr, who merely nodded. They all knew that Pimplemuss wasn't eligible to run for Serene Queen until she had liberated a planet from tyranny. She'd been dragging her friends about the universe for a long time, looking for a hapless planet to liberate. It was the hardest merit badge of all for a Fixipuddling to earn. It was hard on her friends, too.

"What I wonder," said Pimplemuss, "is about those little secret agents in everybody's house. Those nosy bears and tattletale babies and spying little soldiers!"

"I couldn't say," said Foomie. "But for my money, that Lois seems *clever*."

"She seems nasty," said Droyd, "just like Peppa."

"I like her," said Peppa. "I think she's brave and sassy."

"She may be that," said Pimplemuss, "but if that Santa Claws is on his way here tonight, she's going to get chewed up and spit out like nobody's business. We'd better protect her while we can. Let's go hide ourselves in this patch of woods nearby. We can keep out of sight and still be within hearing distance of Lois."

8

Not a Creature Was Stirring, Except Bigfoot

Sammy Grubb was disappointed. The parking lot of the Grand Union was deserted and the store was dark. He could peer through the windows and see the rack of tabloids near the checkout counter, but he couldn't buy one of those newspapers. Not till December 26.

He could still see it in his memory, though.

The headline ran: BETTER WATCH OUT: NOT SANTA BUT *BIGFOOT!*

On the right was a photo of a hairy creature, part bear, part gorilla, part linebacker. It was growling at the camera, showing its best side, which wasn't very good.

Sammy had read the story, start to finish, both paragraphs. A young mother had been at home with her baby when she heard a sound at the door. It was Bigfoot! Luckily she had a camera loaded with film sitting right there on the front hall table.

She had snapped this photo to prove her story to the world. Then she grabbed her baby and ran out the back door to the diner down the road. "My heart was in my throat," she told reporters.

The article had been a bit thin on information. It didn't say where this visitation took place. Or what had happened next. But Sammy could see pine trees in the open doorway behind Bigfoot. And Vermont had its share of pine trees. Probably the newspaper was suppressing the name of the location so the local populace wouldn't panic.

Sammy Grubb knew that these newspapers were a little silly. Sometimes he laughed at the headlines. "I WAS ABDUCTED BY ALIENS!"—words yelled in a speech bubble coming from the mouth of a bald man. And another headline: ELVIS CURED MY CHILBLAINS . . . THEN VANISHED! And how about TALKING DOLPHINS IN THE AFTERLIFE TELL JEANE DIXON: YOU'RE ALL WET!

Sure, it was hard to stomach some of this stuff. But somehow the Bigfoot story seemed more believable. Maybe because, just a month ago, Sammy and the other members of his class had all met a family of ghosts of mastodons. If there could be such a thing as elephant ghosts, why not Bigfoot?

Sammy had wanted to buy the paper so he could study the photo. He wanted to memorize exactly what Bigfoot looked like. Glumly, Sammy turned away from the store window and headed home.

After a while he left the road and plunged into Foggy Hollow, the tree-choked ravine that eventually ran up behind his house. In the spring and summer and fall, Foggy Hollow was a shortcut into his back yard. He could zip from the Josiah Fawcett Elementary School right through Foggy Hollow and end up at his tree house, which served as the headquarters of the Copycats. Or he could pound up the steps onto his back porch and in the back door.

In the winter, however, with snow drifted into the ravine, Foggy Hollow was more of a longcut than a shortcut. Still, Sammy Grubb persevered. His appetite to see Bigfoot was huge.

"Oh, Bigfoot," said Sammy Grubb. He stood still for a moment and looked at the snow-lined branches arched against the cloudy night sky. He felt as if something magical was about to happen. "If only I could see you just once, I think I would know what perfect bliss felt like."

This would be a great time for a creature to emerge and fulfill Sammy's earthly dreams.

Sammy cleared his throat. "I mean, if I could see you *right now*," he clarified.

A small wind came up. A plop of snow fell from a branch.

"Make my Christmas wish come true," whispered Sammy Grubb.

A voice from the bushes said, "What is he *nattering* about? My feet aren't all that big—"

Sammy screamed like a wild thing and took off.

He pounded up the steps to his back porch. He nearly tore the storm door off its hinges. He flung himself inside.

"What's the uproar all about?" said his dad, munching on some ribbon candy.

Sammy couldn't speak. He had just been granted his wish—Bigfoot had shown up in Foggy Hollow—and he, Samuel Lemuel Grubb, had blown it by being scared. He was too ashamed for words. He didn't deserve to be Chief of the Copycats! He would have to resign.

Either that, or go back and find Bigfoot.

"You're not going out again at this hour, it's Christmas Eve," said his mother. "We have to trim the tree." She put on a tape of Perry Como singing Christmas songs.

"Mom," said Sammy. But he knew it was hopeless. Christmas always bulldozed everything in its path.

9

Here Comes Santa Claws!

After her students had gone, Miss Earth and her mother straightened up the classroom a bit. "Why not come back to the house for a little treat?" said Grandma Earth to Mayor Timothy Grass.

Mayor Grass had a soft spot in his heart for Miss Earth, so he said yes. Still in his Santa Claus costume, he drove his old Dodge Dart behind Grandma Earth's Ford pickup.

Grandma Earth unlocked the door to Grandma Earth's Baked Goods and Auto Repair Shop, which was attached to the house she shared with her daughter. Grandma Earth collected some gingerbread men in a piece of wax paper. The three friends sat in the parlor and nibbled on gingerbread and sipped eggnog with a little something added to give it some zip. Miss Earth was feeling a lot better; she sneezed only eighteen times.

Mayor Grass said, "Is it really a problem for you,

Germaine, that the boys and girls have rival clubs?"

"Oh," said Miss Earth, "they're good kids. But there's something about a club I don't approve of. A club is fine if you're in it, but not so fine if you're not. And clubs can lead to a pack mentality. Members following the orders of their leader. Frankly, I prefer students to be individuals."

"Pearl doesn't belong to either club," said Grandma Earth.

"Pearl is a sensible child," said Miss Earth. "She's got her mind on other things. Having five sisters and a brother keeps her busy enough. It's almost like having a club of your own, belonging to such a big family."

"But you don't have any *serious* problem with the kids being in clubs," said Mayor Grass. "They're not vandals. They don't misbehave. None of that dangerous stuff."

"Oh, no," said Miss Earth. "Heavens no. It's all in fun at the heart of it. It's just that I prefer kids to think for themselves. You know, democracy rests on the power of the common citizen to think for himself."

"Or herself," said Mayor Grass. Miss Earth smiled at him. In grammar, as in life, she appreciated equal opportunity. Mayor Grass felt dizzy and fizzy at her smile. He finished his gingerbread man and said, "I trust the common citizen. Why shouldn't I? I've never lost an election in my life. I've been mayor for three consecutive terms."

"And a fine mayor, too," said Grandma Earth. "What I like about you is that you care about everybody in town, not just the voters. You care about the kids and the farm animals and the tourists and the wildlife. You're kind of cute, too. I wish you were a bit more mature. I mean in age. You're too young for me."

Mayor Grass put on his Santa Claus beard to hide his blush at the compliment. Then he thanked his hostesses for the treat. But when he went out to his car, the engine wouldn't start.

"Wouldn't you know it!" he grumbled.

Grandma Earth and Miss Earth were standing in the open doorway of the garage. When they heard the mayor's car engine stutter and die, they came forward.

"Put that baby in neutral and we'll push her back in the bay," said Grandma Earth, rolling up her holiday shirtsleeves. "Germaine, sweetie, would you move those tire rims out of the way? Don't worry, Tim, we'll give you a jump start and you'll be chirking along home in five minutes."

"Grandma Earth," said Mayor Grass, "this old junk heap has been giving me battery trouble for a month. I should have a new one—"

"Nothing easier!" said Grandma Earth. "Let me just climb into my overalls and get me a spanner, and—"

"Grandma, it's nearly midnight on Christmas Eve," said Mayor Grass. "I know you were planning to go to the midnight service at church. This repair can wait. I'll walk home. Look, it's started to snow—it's a lovely night for a walk. Germaine, you make sure your mother behaves, now. Get her to church."

"Mother, he's right," said Miss Earth. "Christmas comes but once a year, and you always like the music at midnight Mass."

"A neighbor in need gets my help if I can give it," said Grandma Earth stoutly.

"But I'm not in need, not really. It's only a mile or two," said Mayor Grass. "Do me some good after all those yummies. No, you two hurry on to church, and I'll enjoy the snowflakes."

"What about your Santa Claus costume?" said Grandma Earth. "Is that red velvet? It'll be ruined."

"It's red flannel, not velvet. Nothing much can hurt red flannel. Don't worry about me. I'll be fine. Say hi to Father Fogarty for me." Mayor Grass leaned back and put his white-gloved hands on his black-belted waist. "Ho ho ho! Merry Christmas to all, and to all a good night!" Then he waved at his friends and disappeared into the night.

"What a good mayor we have," said Grandma Earth warmly. "He's not married, you know, dearie."

"He's a very good mayor," said Miss Earth, a bit primly. "It's Christmas Eve, Mother, not Valentine's Day. We'll just about make it to church on time if we hurry. Get your hat and coat."

*

Mayor Grass *was* a good mayor. He loved the village of Hamlet, Vermont. Viewed from Grandma Earth's Baked Goods and Auto Body Shop, the village had a cheery aspect, like calendar pictures of Vermont Life in Winter. The snow fell with a grainy, shushing sound. The white pines and the maples and walnuts and birches seemed like gentle spirits poised in a game of freeze tag, waiting for him to pass. He liked walking at night. He never read Stephen King novels, so he wasn't scared at all.

As he strolled along, he swung his arms boisterously to get warm. He passed a family walking to church. "Evening, Santa Claus," they said respectfully.

"Evening, good folks of Hamlet," said Mayor Grass with a twinkle in his eye.

"Mommy, is that really Santa Claus?" he heard one of the little ones say. "Where's his sleigh?"

"Probably getting a tune-up over at Grandma Earth's," said the mother. "You can trust Grandma Earth to fix anything."

Mayor Grass smiled. He didn't mind pretending to be Santa Claus once a year. It was part of the job of being mayor.

But he wouldn't mind being home soon. He would light his pipe, put on his carpet slippers, and dip into the next chapter of his suspense thriller, *Helpless in Hollywood.* It was about a U.S. president who gets kidnapped by a Hollywood starlet with a deranged attitude toward the government.

Mayor Grass was at a really good part. The Hollywood starlet, named Spangles O'Leary, had tied up the president to a straight-backed chair. Then she had dressed herself up in a skimpy pink satin gown showing an awful lot of what she called her credentials, the likes of which are rarely seen in cabinet meetings. Spangles O'Leary wanted to audition for a role as secretary of state. Under the president's chair she had placed a bunch of dynamite with lit fuses sticking out. The president had five minutes to agree to give her a cabinet post or he was history.

Mayor Grass was so intent on getting home to finish *Helpless in Hollywood* that at first he didn't hear the sound of scuffling. When he did notice the noise at last, he thought it was the Kennedys' dog, Reebok, out sniffing for frozen squirrels or something. He hoped Reebok wouldn't bark or snarl at him.

"Nice doggie," said Mayor Grass, a little nervously. "Nice doggie."

A small voice came from just beyond the lip of the ravine. "On the count of four! Three! One! Two! *Whatever!*"

Suddenly the mayor was bewildered by—by what? A group of stout kindergartners? They came rushing out from Foggy Hollow and threw themselves at him. "Happy holidays . . ." began the mayor uneasily. But one of the tykes had tackled him by the ankles, locking his legs together, and two others were pulling his hands behind his back.

Mayor Grass tried to scramble away. No luck. They all rolled in the snow. It was like a World Wrestling Federation championship for midgets. Mayor Grass managed to get to his feet, but they were all over him again.

"Death to the tyrant!" came a voice from a chubby little thing—no kindergartner, now he could see, but a little Munchkin of some sort, with yellow-white braids and rosy cheeks. "Or, if not death, then some sort of clever torture, like pulling out your beard hair by hair!"

"Ooh, how horrible! Pimplemuss, you're disgusting!" said one of the dwarfy-things.

"Or—or—or kicking you in the stomach a hundred times!" said the Pimplemuss creature, demonstrating a violence rarely seen in Vermont, Christmas Eve or not.

"Look at that fat stomach! You thrive by stealing the food of your poor downtrodden subjects!" said another one.

"Or worse yet," said Pimplemuss, fixing Mayor Grass with a beady eye, "we'll torture you by *tickling*!"

True, Mayor Grass had the stomach for reading frightening suspense stories in the middle of the night. But he had no stomach for tickling. He fainted dead away. Right on top of Foomie.

"Get off me, you tub of lard," moaned Foomie.

"I didn't come to Earth to be flattened by an old fathead."

"We've got him!" shouted Peppa and Droyd, jumping up and down. "What should we do with him now?"

"If he has spies everywhere, someone may be watching," declared Pimplemuss. "We mustn't give them a chance to rescue him. So back to the starship *Loiterbug*. On the double!"

They hoisted him overhead and carried him away.

10

Jingle Bell Shock

Mayor Grass awoke with a funny feeling in his head. It felt as if he had been out on a date with a sledgehammer. "Ho ho ho," he said uneasily.

"Hey," said a voice, "so our disgusting guest is waking up. Well, all I can say, Your Most Unlikableness, the Right Dishonorable Supreme Dictator, Mister Santa Claws, is: Welcome to your downfall if not your doom."

Mayor Grass blinked his eyes several times. He looked about.

He was lying on a purple blanket spread out over a floor made of steel mesh. He could see through the floor to the level below, which housed some odd-looking machinery. It looked like a cross between a giant popcorn maker and an automobile engine.

Was he suffering from delusion? Jingle bell shock? Too much holiday eggnog? "Where am I?"

he said. "And who are you?" He sat up. Were his hands tied behind his back? Yes, they were.

Five little creatures were standing before him. They were dressed like—like Santa's elves. Red and green clothes, cheery gold piping, ribbons and buckles and bows.

"I'm Pimplemuss," said the leader. She had nut-brown eyes and a dimpled cheek, but her expression was grim and probing. Mayor Grass had to glance away.

There was a man with a long white beard that looked as if it were fluttering in the wind—though there was no wind. "That is Narr," said Pimplemuss. Narr took a bow in Mayor Grass's direction. Narr's beard flew up and covered his face shyly the way a bib will sometimes cover a baby's face—only the bib usually doesn't decide to do this on its own.

"And this is Foomie," said Pimplemuss, indicating a strange thing that looked like a fountain of golden hair without a face.

Foomie made a movement that was halfway between a curtsy and a bow, and fell over. "Standing on two feet, it's so difficult," came a voice from inside the hair.

"Finally, the little ones," said Pimplemuss. The two who looked most like children batted their eyes and stared at their feet. "Droyd, straighten up and put your shoulders back when I introduce you. Peppa, take your thumb out of your mouth. Say good morning to Mister Santa Claws."

"Good morning, Mister Santa Claws," said Droyd and Peppa in unison.

"Can it be Christmas morning already?" said Mayor Grass. He sat up. "Am I having a dream? Did I go to sleep reading *Helpless in Hollywood* and is this the result? Are you going to blow me up with dynamite?"

"Now, that's a helpful idea we never thought of," said Foomie.

Mayor Grass made a mental note not to be so helpful in the future.

"I'm dreaming. Are you Santa's little helpers?" he said. He looked around at the blinking lights and the high-tech equipment. "I always thought the North Pole would be a little bit more like Switzerland, with the smell of gingerbread baking, and hot cocoa, and everything made out of candy canes and lollipops. More Play-Skool than Sharper Image. Well, live and learn."

Then he shook his head. "Boy, I'm really out of it. What am I saying? There's no such thing as Santa Claus."

"Yeah, right," said Pimplemuss. "If you say so, Mister Santa Claws. Now be quiet and listen. We don't have time for this chatter. It won't be long before your spies are out looking for you. So we need to know just how we can persuade you to give up on your life of crime and terror."

"Crime and terror?" said Mayor Grass. "I only *read* about crime and terror. I don't practice them."

"Hah!" said Pimplemuss. "As if you expect us to believe that!"

"No, I'm the mayor of this village," said Mayor Grass. "Did you think you had captured the real Santa Claus?"

"He's trying to fool us," said Pimplemuss. "Everyone, stand firm!"

"Pull the hairs from his beard!" cried Foomie, nipping up and jerking out a long white hair. The prisoner didn't even flinch.

"Kick him in the stomach!" cried Foomie. Then, giving a wild interstellar scream of energy, Foomie lunged forward and kickboxed the prisoner in his fat stomach. The stomach—which was mostly pillows—merely shook a bit from side to side, sort of like a bowl full of jelly.

"My," said Foomie. "Impressive."

Mayor Grass said, "What a *strange* dream this is!"

"Time," bellowed Pimplemuss, "for the tickle-fest!"

The five elves rushed at Mayor Grass and began to tickle him all over. He fell back on the purple blanket and began to shriek. "No! No! Please! Anything—any—anything but this!" His giggles rose hysterically; his limbs thrashed.

"You are Santa Claws, aren't you?" yelled Pimplemuss. "Confess it!"

Mayor Grass couldn't stand to be tickled. "Please! Yes! I am Santa—I confess! Just st-st-stop! Oh, ho ho ho! Ho ho ho!"

"Enough," said Pimplemuss at once. "I don't believe in beating a creature when he's down, even if he's an evil old dictator."

While he was trying to catch his breath, Mayor Grass's mind raced to make some sense of this predicament. If he could feel himself being tickled, then he wasn't dreaming. But who could these little fiends be? There was no such thing as elves. But they sure looked like elves.

It was best, thought Mayor Grass, to be as honest as possible. He said, "I don't believe you little folks could mistake me for Santa Claus. There is no Santa Claus. What planet are you from, anyway?"

"Fixipuddle," blurted out Droyd, just as Pimplemuss was saying, "Don't anybody give it away . . ."

"Fixipuddle?" said Mayor Grass. "You're not *really* from another planet?"

"Mister Santa Claws," said Pimplemuss, coming forward, "we may not have much time. Your secret service may be on our trail even as we speak. We're going to have to ask you to step down from your role as Supreme Fat Guy on the planet. But we're reasonable. We don't mean to do you harm. We only want to ask you for one thing before we let you go."

"What's that?" said Mayor Grass. "Anything!"

"We want you to lead us to your Fortress of Fear," said Pimplemuss, "so we can free the elves from their slavery. We want to dismantle your factory that makes secret agent spies in the shape of babies and bears and little soldiers. Then all on this planet can breathe the air of freedom. We'll find someone to give us a testimonial letter that says we liberated your planet. When that is done, we will let you go. On this cold planet, you can live out the remainder of your days, turning into an old, bitter man, reflecting on your crimes."

"You are completely bananas," said Mayor Grass. He was beginning to get annoyed. "I don't have any Fortress of Fear. I live in an apartment above the old Hay and Feed Shop, which is now the Vermont Museum of Interesting Facts to Know and Tell."

"Know this, fattypants," snarled Pimplemuss. "You lead us to your Fortress of Fear or we'll zip you out of this planet so fast your beard will fall off! And *don't think we can't do it!*"

"Actually, Pimplemuss," mumbled Foomie from the control panels, "I'm not sure we *can* do it. Don't forget we seem to have jostled some machinery in that unfortunate landing . . ."

"I can show you the Vermont Museum of Interesting Facts to Know and Tell," said Mayor Grass with enthusiasm. If he could only get out of here, he could call the state police. But who would believe him? "Help, I've been captured by five aliens who look like insane elves from Santa's Toyland over at the Ethantown Mall?" The fellows in the state police would think he'd gone mad.

They'd say, "Tim, too much nutmeg in the eggnog, for sure."

He had to get out. He noticed that Peppa and Droyd were looking interested. He said, "There are lots of displays at the museum. I could show you the famous two-headed chicken that showed up out of an egg on Cowflop Farm over in Puster Center. The two heads used to go for the same bit of chicken feed. They played chicken with each other, if you know what I mean. It's really fun."

"What's *fun?*" said Peppa.

"Fun. You know, *fun* fun," said Mayor Grass. "Fun is . . . when you like something so much you don't realize how much time is passing."

"Please, can we go, Pimplemuss?" wheedled Droyd.

"I want to see a statue of a two-headed chicken," whined Peppa. "What's a chicken, anyway?"

"We're not going anywhere," said Pimplemuss. "He's just playing for time."

"We never get to go anywhere," said Droyd.

"We never get to do anything," said Peppa.

"Actually, I wouldn't mind a little outing myself," began Foomie.

"SILENCE!" roared Pimplemuss. In a lower voice, she said, "You want a standoff, Santa Claws— well, we can wait. We're not going anywhere. We'll keep you here until you promise to bring us to the Fortress of Fear. We can wait for a thousand years if necessary."

11

Tattletales on Red Alert

After midnight Mass, Grandma Earth felt a surge of energy. She kissed her daughter good night. Then, sipping a little leftover eggnog and humming "Joy to the World," she went to work, replacing the bad battery in Mayor Grass's old Dodge Dart. Within forty minutes the car was purring like new.

In the morning, after Grandma Earth whipped up a Bavarian strudel with sour cherry filling, she and her daughter exchanged presents. Grandma Earth gave Germaine a flannel nightie and a paperback book called *Men: How to Find 'Em, How to Tell If They're Ripe, How to Keep 'Em*. Miss Earth was insulted until she realized it was a joke book. "As if men ever really ripen!" she said, teasing her mother. "That's a good one!"

Miss Earth gave her mother a flannel nightie too, as well as a new pan for baking French bread and a subscription to *The Jalopy Quarterly Review.*

In the late morning, Grandma Earth said, "Honey, I think I'll drive Tim's car back home for him. Would you follow me in the pickup and bring me back?"

"Yes," said Miss Earth. "We can give him some of this leftover strudel."

"As a baker, I object to the word *leftover,*" said Grandma Earth. "I prefer *moreover.* But it's a good idea." She wrapped a generous portion in a checkered tea towel and put the whole thing in a wicker basket.

When Grandma Earth pulled into Mayor Grass's side yard—which was also the parking lot for the Vermont Museum of Interesting Facts to Know and Tell—she noticed something strange. She gestured to her daughter to turn off the motor of the pickup and roll down the window.

"Look, Germaine," said Grandma Earth. "It appears that Tim never came home last night."

"What do you mean?" said Miss Earth, but then she saw. "Oh—the fresh snow on the side porch. There are no footprints in it."

"It was snowing when Tim left us last night," said Grandma Earth. "But it stopped soon thereafter. And it wasn't a windy night, so Tim's footprints couldn't have been filled in by drifting snow. Do you think something has happened to him?" She rang the doorbell, then opened the door and called up the steps, "Morning, Tim, Merry

Christmas! Halloooo!" But there was no answer, and the house was stone cold.

"Mother, don't pry," said Miss Earth. "Perhaps someone gave him a lift, or maybe he had plans to visit someone after he left us. It's none of our business."

"I'm going up," said Grandma Earth. "I have to leave his keys on the table anyway."

She came back a moment later. "No one there. No sign of his Santa Claus costume. Who could he have been visiting at such a late hour on Christmas Eve?"

"Mother, it's none of our business," Miss Earth reminded her.

"Still," said Grandma Earth. "He left our house at half an hour to midnight. Let's just make a few phone calls when we get home."

"Well, all right," said Miss Earth. "Please, though, let's not alarm anyone."

But it was too late. Alarm had already taken hold.

A figure was slinking back around the corner of the building. In the harsh light of sun on snow, it kept to the blue-black shadows. It pulled its man's fedora down over its brow and adjusted its dark glasses. It was Lois Kennedy the Third. Her Christmas wish had come true.

She was decked out in trench coat, snap-brimmed hat, and sunglasses. She had a magnifying glass in one pocket and a flashlight in the other. A Swiss army knife was attached to one of the loops on her belt. The only thing wrong with the picture was her red plastic boots, but she couldn't help that. Her mom wouldn't let her go outside without boots.

Lois Kennedy the Third was so excited that she almost forgot to keep to the shadows. She hurried home. This was the opportunity of a lifetime! She burst into her house, knocking her little brother off his new rocking horse. "Whoopsie," she said, "sorry," and lifted him back up. Her mom and dad were still nibbling on breakfast bacon and reading the paper.

"Whoa, there's a spy in a hurry," said her dad.

"Gotta use the phone," said Lois. "Gotta call the gang."

"Lois," said her mom, "this is Christmas. It's a day to spend with your family. Don't go pestering your friends. You can call them tomorrow."

"I can't afford to squander this chance, Mom," said Lois. She faced her mother squarely and whipped off her dark glasses. "It's like this. Once in a lifetime an opportunity comes down the pike. You recognize it, you seize it, your life is changed forever. If you don't seize it, you're doomed to play second fiddle on the wrong side of the tracks for the rest of your two-bit no-account sour-grapes life."

"I worry about you sometimes," said her mother.

"Empress Lois Kennedy the Third?" said Lois.

"Or classic nobody-in-a-nutshell? It comes down to that."

She bounded up the stairs. Her parents looked at each other with raised eyebrows and tried to stifle some giggles. They didn't realize how serious this was.

Lois made some quick phone calls: Fawn Petros. Sharday Wren. Anna Maria Mastrangelo. Carly Garfunkel. Nina Bueno. All the girls answered. All the girls agreed to come over.

Then Lois thought: How do I secure an advantage over Thekla? By bringing in an unknown element. So Lois dialed the number of Pearl Hotchkiss, the only girl in class who wasn't a Tattletale. But nobody answered. Then Lois remembered that last night the Hotchkiss family had gone off to Connecticut for the holidays. Darn!

Oh, well. Couldn't be helped. The last phone call was to Thekla Mustard. The current and soon-to-be-former Empress of the Tattletales.

"Thekla?" said Lois Kennedy the Third sweetly. "It's Lois. Yeah yeah, merry merry, happy happy, all that stuff. Look. I'm calling an emergency session of the Tattletales at my house for this afternoon. Two P.M. sharp. Be there or suffer the consequences."

Lois listened to the squawking and sputtering. Then she said, "Thekla, I know I'm not authorized to call a meeting. I'm doing it anyway. This is Red

Alert. This is a catastrophe of epic proportions."
She slammed the phone down. It was a satisfying
slam. Then she went downstairs to get a peanut
butter sandwich. She needed the protein. She had
to plan her campaign.

✳

At 2 P.M. sharp, a rap came on the kitchen door.
Lois said hi to the gang, who came in and shucked
their boots, coats, mittens, scarves, and hats. Nina,
Carly, Anna Maria, Sharday, and Fawn. Where was
Thekla?

But there she was, running down the road. She
pirouetted inside, past the others, and threw off
her winter coat with a flourish.

Oooh, she's good, Lois thought. Can't deny that.

Thekla Mustard, the long-standing Empress of
the Tattletales, wasn't about to give up her authority without a fight. That much was certain.

Though Thekla didn't know the reason for the
emergency meeting, she could guess that Lois was
challenging her leadership as Empress. So Thekla
had taken steps. She was dressed in a natty minia-
ture business suit with a power bow perking up the
neckline. She carried an efficient-looking clipboard. A pen was attached to it with dental floss.

Before Lois had the chance to say a word,
Thekla flipped open a note pad clipped onto the
clipboard, and she said, "Let's see, in alphabetical
order: Nina Bueno, Carly Garfunkel, Lois Kennedy

the Third, Anna Maria Mastrangelo, Fawn Petros, and Sharday Wren. Here, here, here, here, here, here. And *moi*: Thekla Mustard, Empress of the Tattletales. *Here.*" She underlined her own name with a curvy stroke and smacked the clipboard briskly. "Let's get started, shall we?"

"Glad you could come," said Lois, trying to regain some ground.

"Glad to take charge," said Thekla. She marched into the family room and said to Lois's little brother, "*You.* Up and out. Party's over. We need this space. Go to Mama." She lifted Lois's little brother off his new rocking horse. He stood in the doorway of the room with his eyes wide open, and then he ran for safety.

Thekla settled herself in the wicker chair with the huge back, framing herself nicely in it. Lois had meant to sit there herself. Darn! But she wasn't going to let Thekla get away with this.

"We have a serious problem in this town," said Lois. She paused for dramatic emphasis.

"Proceed, Lois, they need to know," said Thekla, indicating the other members of the Tattletales club. "Cut to the chase."

Lois ran her fingers along the lapels of her new trench coat and then sunk her hands deep in the pockets. "I have it on the highest authority that Mr. Timothy Grass, mayor of Hamlet, has disappeared. Sometime in the middle of the night. And our own teacher, Miss Earth, and her mother are the only ones who know about it. Something must be done, and here's what I propose—"

"Wait a minute, Lois." Thekla had her eyes down in her notebook, glancing through some scribbled thoughts. "From where did he disappear?"

"He was last seen by Grandma Earth and Miss Earth at eleven-thirty last night. He said good-bye to them following a party and headed home. But he never arrived. This much is certain."

"How do you know?" said Thekla.

"I don't reveal my sources," said Lois bravely.

Thekla stood. She recognized a leadership challenge when she saw one. "Lois Kennedy the Third," she said, "I shall call this meeting to a close at once if you don't tell us how you came upon this information."

"Very well," said Lois, making the best of a bad situation. "You'll have noticed my new spy outfit."

Each girl said, "Ooooh," and wished she'd got one too.

"Well, this morning I was passing the Vermont Museum of Interesting Facts to Know and Tell when I heard a vehicle pull into the yard, and then another. Grandma Earth was driving Mayor Grass's car, and Miss Earth was following in the pickup. For practice, I hid myself and overheard Miss Earth and her mother talking about Mayor Grass being missing."

"Thank you for your honesty—" said Thekla.

"Furthermore—" began Lois.

"—and for your brevity," said Thekla, smiling thinly. "Now, girls, here's what we do." Lois's jaw dropped open. Even in her own home, she couldn't outdo Thekla Mustard!

"Not a word to a soul," Thekla ordered. "Check every garage, every barn, every basement, every attic. Invent any excuse you must. Knock on your neighbors' doors and ask discreet questions. But never, ever, ever breathe a word about your intentions. We wouldn't want to turn this Christmas into a carnival of crisis. Call in what you find to me. Lois," said Thekla, perking up her power bow as she spoke, "you have done good work. You are a credit to the Tattletales, the foremost club in Hamlet, Vermont, and also, I daresay, in the universe as we know it."

The meeting was over. The girls left. Lois was disgruntled and annoyed. Still, even she did what she was told.

She retraced her own steps to the edge of Foggy Hollow, where she had said good night to Sammy Grubb. There, at the edge of the ravine, she came upon a clue. The red Santa Claus hat with the white pom-pom stitched onto the tip. It lay like a bloody scar against the white snow.

Lois's blood ran cold. She snatched up the hat and raced home.

12

Hysteria in Hamlet

It was all very well for Thekla Mustard to tell her subjects to keep a secret. But this secret was too horrible to keep. Mayor Grass was too beloved of the folks of Hamlet, Vermont. By suppertime the news was all over town.

Pastor Rebecca Mopp rang the bell of the Unitarian Church for an emergency meeting there. Even Father Fogarty left his own church down the road—Saint Mary in the Tombstones—with all the lights still blazing. "If Tim Grass could only see how many friends he has in Hamlet," said Father Fogarty, "he'd receive a very nice Christmas present indeed."

Grandma Earth convened the meeting. "Good neighbors of Hamlet," she cried, "perhaps there is a simple explanation for Tim's disappearance. But for now, we can't afford to take chances."

Widow Wendell stood up and called, "Grandma

Earth, Tim was expected at my boardinghouse for Christmas brunch today—it's called the Lovey Inn, singles start at twenty-five dollars a night in the off-season as you all know—and he never showed up. Nor did he call."

Everybody shivered and whispered. Grandma Earth gulped. Miss Earth leaped to her side. "Dear friends!" she trumpeted. "This is *not* the time to panic! We must climb every mountain and ford every stream! We must follow every lead, however insignificant!"

"Miss Earth is right, as always!" said Mr. Grubb.

"But we have no clues!" called Mrs. Cobble, knitting away at a potholder.

"*Wrong!*" came a voice. They all turned to look.

From the back of the Unitarian Church came a vision in a trench coat, dark glasses, a fedora, and a pair of red plastic boots, leading Reebok on a leash. Lois strode up the center aisle until she arrived in front of the podium.

"Permission to address the crowd?" she said.

"By all means," said Grandma Earth.

Lois Kennedy the Third whipped off her hat and glasses. "I have reason to believe that Mayor Grass fell into harm's way somewhere near Foggy Hollow."

"And why is that?" said Grandma Earth.

Lois said, "I understand that last night he left Grandma's Baked Goods and Auto Repair Shop and was walking home. Well, you should know that

74

this afternoon I found a clue indicating a possible struggle. Maybe Mayor Grass ran into some troublemakers."

"But who could it be?" called Widow Wendell.

"There are several possibilities," said Lois. "The first is highway robbers."

"Squished Toad Road isn't near the interstate," said Miss Earth. "Let's not get fanciful, Lois."

"The second is teenage punks," said Lois.

"We don't have teenage punks in Hamlet, Vermont," said Miss Earth. "Really, Lois, nobody I ever taught could grow up to be a punk."

"That's true," Lois agreed. "I take it back. That leaves the only other possibility, which I admit is farfetched."

"Which is?" said Miss Earth.

"Bigfoot," said Lois.

"Oh, Lois," said Miss Earth. "Have you been listening to Sammy Grubb? Bigfoot is only a legend. It doesn't exist. But even if it did, and if it got into a scuffle with someone or something near Foggy Hollow, how do we know it was with Mayor Grass?"

Lois held up the Santa Claus hat.

Miss Earth clutched the side of the podium with fingers of steel. Grandma Earth said darkly, "Well, nonsense about Bigfoot aside, we'd better have a look-see."

"Follow me!" shouted Lois.

They raced out of the church. The place where Foggy Hollow met Squished Toad Road wasn't far.

Before long three or four dozen people were standing at the side of Squished Toad Road, a few feet away from where Lois had found the cap. There was no doubt at all that there had been a fight. Even though a light dusting had fallen, you could still see the snow beneath had been disturbed.

Grandma Earth said, "But how can we tell which way they went from here? The road has been scraped with snowplows."

Lois Kennedy the Third said, "I don't know if Mayor Grass wore the Santa Claus hat often enough to leave an odor, but we can try. Here, Reebok! Come on, boy!"

Reebok sniffed the hat inside and out. He looked puzzled. Then he went and sniffed where the scuffle had been. He looked more puzzled. Then he took off.

"Attaboy!" shouted Lois.

The neighbors and friends followed at a clip.

Reebok could run fast. In forty seconds he had outpaced them all and disappeared from view.

"We should have brought our cars," said Grandma Earth. "That was stupid of us."

They trudged along the road, past Old Man Fingerpie's farm, past the turnoff for Ethan Allen Park, all the way back into town. No sign of Reebok anywhere. In the end, the friends and neighbors went back to the Unitarian Church and divided the town up into quadrants. Then they did what the

Tattletales had done earlier that day. They searched the town high and low.

Jasper Stripe, the school janitor, even had a look in Old Man Fingerpie's barn. But he never noticed the starship *Loiterbug* crashed in a heap next to the barn, because sometime during the night the snow on the barn roof had slid off in a big heap and covered the starship. Jasper Stripe assumed it was just a big mound of hay.

By 9 P.M., when the villagers met again at the church hall, they were in no mood for the hot cider and gingerbread men that Mrs. Cobble and Mrs. Brill had set out.

The adults were busy wondering if they should call the state police or the FBI. "Look," said Lois, holding up a gingerbread man whose lower part had bloated from too much cookie dough. "Bigfoot."

Nobody even smiled. They were too depressed. It was not a very Christmasy-feeling Christmas. "Oh, wherever you are," murmured Miss Earth, staring at the big-footed cookie Lois had given her, "I hope you're safe."

Lois had the feeling that Miss Earth wasn't really talking to the gingerbread man.

13

Reebok and the Alien Elves

Reebok trooped off down the road with the faint smell of Mayor Timothy Grass's frozen socks in his nostrils.

Reebok's nose was smart. When Reebok sniffed at the hat, here's what he thought about:

The kind of shampoo Mayor Grass had used that day. The kind of detergent the hat had been cleaned in a week earlier.

The most recent scent was of grosbeak claw, left when a yellow grosbeak had alighted on the hat where it had fallen on the ground. The grosbeak had stood there in order to think about what to do next in life. (Eat or fly. Big choice.)

The strongest scent, however, was the odor of human sweat from Mayor Grass's scalp. Reebok easily could separate this essential aroma from the others. It was simple when your nose was so talented.

So Reebok loped down Squished Toad Road.

His nose was set on SEARCH. There were some pretty neat smells here and there, odors of things left behind on the roadside by other passing animals. Reebok allowed himself to indulge in an occasional snort of something ripe and memorable. He believed that, along life's way, one should take time to stop and smell the roses, so to speak. But after a whiff, he hurried on.

It wasn't long before Reebok got to Old Man Fingerpie's farm. About thirty years ago, Old Man Fingerpie had kept pigs, and Reebok lost himself in a reverie over the smell of pigs who had died long before he was born. His nose crinkled in a pleasurable nostalgia for opportunities missed, and then Reebok remembered his mission. He had found his target! Mayor Grass!

Reebok had a smart nose. But the rest of him wasn't so smart. He didn't think to check and make sure that the posse was still with him. He just barked and barked.

*

Inside the starship *Loiterbug*, Pimplemuss said, "What did that other human Earthling mean, that one we saw in the woods? He said, 'Oh, Bigfoot, if only I could see you once, I should know perfect bliss!' How could he know we have big feet when we're not done up like little Earthling elves?"

"That sounds like Sammy Grubb to me," said

Mayor Grass. "Your normal, red-blooded, monster-craving schoolboy." Then he thought of something else. "What do you mean, 'done up like elves'"? Isn't this the way you really look?"

"Hah! As if," said Pimplemuss.

"So how do you usually—"

"Shh!" said Pimplemuss. "There's that creature again!" They heard barking outside.

The others froze. "What's he saying?" said Foomie at last.

Pimplemuss frowned. Finally she said, "Maybe there's more than one setting on this WordSearch dial." She flipped a lever and pressed in a code. "I think," she said, listening carefully to the barking, "I think he's saying something like, 'Well, what do you know about this!'"

"He'll draw attention to us," said Foomie. "We'd better kidnap him, too."

"You wouldn't kidnap a dog!" said Mayor Grass. "A dog is somebody's *pet*!"

"What's a pet?" said Droyd.

"A creature to love and cherish and have fun with."

"Oh goodie, a pet!" said Droyd.

Foomie said, "What's a dog? Another kind of Earthling?"

"A pet! Perhaps now we'll experience some *fun*," said Peppa. She and her little brother jumped up and down, screaming "Fun! Fun! Fun!"

"Yes, I guess a dog is an Earthling," said Mayor

Grass wearily. "I mean, dogs live on Earth same as human beings."

"Dogs, humans, elves—there are lots of kinds of Earthlings, we're learning," said Pimplemuss. "Well, I'm going to bring the dog in. But don't you get attached to him." Pimplemuss glared at the young Fixipuddlings. "This is a temporary measure."

"We'll love him more than anything in the universe," said Peppa breathlessly.

"More than me?" said Pimplemuss, in a rage.

"Of course not," said Droyd, but not convincingly.

Pimplemuss opened the door of the starship *Loiterbug*. Outside it was dark and cold, and the sound of the barking dog grew louder. "Oh, all right, I hear what you're saying," said Pimplemuss crossly. "Shut up for a moment, won't you?"

"Reebok!" yelled Mayor Grass. "Go, boy! Get help!"

Reebok, smelling the one he was searching for, dashed inside the spaceship with his tail wagging and his tongue out. Pimplemuss slammed the door shut.

Foomie looked doubtful. Narr nibbled his fingernails. "What did you call this tiresome creature of few thoughts?" Pimplemuss said coldly to Mayor Grass.

"He's a dog. A beagle," said Mayor Grass sadly.

Reebok's nose wrinkled. The smells of the alien elves were dive-bombing him from all sides. They

81

didn't smell like anything he'd ever smelled before, except the other night on the way back from the party at the school. And that night the smell had been distilled by the cold mountain air. In here the impact was intense. It smelled of . . . well, no, it was more like . . . on the other hand, wasn't there a hint of . . . ?

Reebok's nose went into overdrive trying to sort it out. Twenty million years of doggie evolution had not prepared him for what he was sniffing. It wasn't bad. It wasn't good. It was just too new to understand. He fell over on his back in a dead faint, with his four feet up in the air.

Droyd and Peppa scratched his stomach. "We love him," said Droyd. "He's our best friend."

"Really," said Pimplemuss coldly.

"He's going to sleep on my bed," said Peppa.

"No, he likes me better," said Droyd.

"You little pip-squeaks, pipe down," said Pimplemuss. "We need to plan our next step. Leave that creature alone."

"I'm going to call him Captain Nose," said Droyd.

"No, his name is Missy," said Peppa.

"His name is Bye-Bye if you don't pipe down!" stormed Pimplemuss.

14

The Boys Believe in Bigfoot

For the next couple of days, there was talk of nothing else but the missing mayor of Hamlet, Vermont.

"I still say," said Miss Earth to her mother, "Mayor Grass got a ride to another village and is having a good time there."

Grandma Earth was mixing bread dough. She said, a little sharply, "He was invited to join Widow Wendell at the Lovey Inn for Christmas brunch. It's not like Tim to forget his social plans."

Then she added, "The Widow Wendell is not half as attractive as you are. But, like you, she's available. So when Mayor Grass shows up again, I wouldn't let my chances pass me by if I were you."

"Mother," said Miss Earth, "haven't you got somebody else's dough to knead?"

✳

There were lots of different theories about what had happened to Mayor Grass, but whatever it was, it seemed to have happened to Reebok, too.

Thekla Mustard called another meeting of the Tattletales. Lois's ideas of highway robbers or teenage punks had not impressed anyone. The idea of Bigfoot was dismissed as being too ridiculous, too dumb; only boys would believe in something so stupid.

Thekla Mustard put forward the notion of time travel. "Wasn't Mayor Grass dressed up as Santa Claus?" said Thekla. "Perhaps he trod on a flaw in the space-time continuum. Maybe he was whisked somewhere into the future to be the Ghost of Christmas Past, like in *A Christmas Carol*."

"Or maybe he's been spirited away somewhere in the past to be the Ghost of Christmas Yet To Come!" said Carly Garfunkel. "It makes a lot of sense!"

"Either way, he's really the Ghost of Christmas Present," said Nina Bueno, and that made them all sniffle a little. Because they all knew and liked Mayor Grass.

"The Ghost of Christmas Presents?" said Fawn Petros. "Does that mean he's the ghost of presents that you got the other day and already broke or used up?"

"Fawn," said Thekla Mustard, "get a life."

*

Across town, the boys in Miss Earth's class were having their own meeting at Sammy Grubb's house. Sammy called the roll of Copycats: Hector Yellow. Mike Saint Michael. Stan Tomaski. Forest Eugene Mopp. Salim Bannerjee. Moshe Cohn.

When all the boys were listening, Sammy told them about his wish for Bigfoot to come to Hamlet, and about the strange noise he heard in the woods on Christmas Eve.

"You're lying. You're pulling our legs," said Stan Tomaski. "Promise?"

"Honest promise," said Sammy Grubb.

"Enough to make the pledge?" asked Mike Saint Michael.

"Enough to make the pledge," said Sammy. He stood up and put his right hand on his heart and said,

> *Cross my heart and hope to die*
> *If what I say should be a lie.*
> *May worms go nuts within my guts*
> *Before another day goes by.*

The other boys stood up solemnly. They put their right hands on their hearts and answered,

> *May maggot flies devour your eyes,*
> *May bees and fleas annoy your knees,*
> *May hornet swarms attack your arms,*
> *May spider eggs infest your legs.*
> *May every creepy crawly who*
> *Needs breakfast, lunch, and dinner too*
> *Go munchy-crunchy-scrunchy through*

The you that there is left to chew
If what you say should prove untrue.

Hector Yellow had written this promise, and he was proud of it. He beamed as Sammy Grubb said his part and the boys said theirs. Once it was all done, the boys had to believe Sammy Grubb.

It wasn't hard to believe their Chief. Besides, they didn't think that the idea of Bigfoot was so stupid. For one thing, where else would Reebok have gone? He could only have been eaten by a snow monster. But was there such a thing?

"Of course there is," said Sammy Grubb. "Look. Fellows. Be real. If there could be such things as Siberian snow spiders and the ghosts of mastodons—both of which we saw with our own eyes—why couldn't there be Bigfoot? Besides, here's this picture in the *National Town Crier*. I bought it at the Grand Union at last."

"But," said Salim, "what, please, is a Bigfoot?"

"It's a monster who lives in the hills," said Forest Eugene Mopp.

"It's the missing link between human beings and Godzilla," said Hector Yellow.

"It's part bear, part gorilla, and part Sumo wrestler," said Stan Tomaski.

"It's like a kind of furry Frankenstein," said Mike Saint Michael.

"No," said Moshe Cohn. "Frankenstein was the doctor who invented the monster. The monster he invented was called Frankenstein's monster."

"But who invented Bigfoot?" said Salim Bannerjee, more puzzled than ever. "Big Hand?"

"No one knows where it comes from or where it goes," said Sammy Grubb. "Some say it lives in the Arctic north and only wanders down into temperate climes when the air is crisp and cold and snow is on the ground—like now. It's been an unusually cold month, even for December."

"Some say it eats human babies for breakfast," said Mike Saint Michael.

"Who says that?" said Sammy Grubb.

"Well, I do," said Mike. "I wish it would come to my house and eat my baby sisters. Boy, can they scream when we run out of Cheerios!"

"Doesn't this look like Vermont?" asked Sammy Grubb. He pointed to the cover of the *National Town Crier.*

"It looks horrible," said Salim.

"Something may have drawn Bigfoot to Hamlet, Vermont," said Sammy Grubb. "Maybe the smell of holiday baking sent him over the edge. In fact, maybe Bigfoot was lurking outside Grandma Earth's Baked Goods and Auto Repair Shop on Christmas Eve! You know how wonderful that place always smells, especially in the winter. Maybe she gave Mayor Grass some cookies or something to take home from the party. Bigfoot smelled the cookies in Mayor Grass's pocket and carried him away."

"And did what?" said Salim, horrified.

"Well," said Sammy Grubb grimly, "let's just

hope that Bigfoot has some workable fingers and opposable thumbs like human beings. Because if he couldn't get the cookies out of Mayor Grass's pocket, I'm afraid he would probably just eat up the mayor and enjoy the faint flavor of cookies."

"A cookie-flavored mayor?" said Salim. "Eaten by Bigfoot the Snow Monster? Oh, this country really *is* a strange and dangerous place to live, just as everybody back in Bombay used to say!"

"But Sammy," said Moshe, "what you heard in the woods was speaking English. How could Bigfoot know English?"

"I don't claim to know," said Sammy. "I'm the Chief of the Copycats, not Professor Sherlock Einstein Holmes. We'll have to keep an open mind until we know for sure."

15

Espionage of the Elves

Mayor Grass strained against his bonds. He wished, he wished, he *wished* he had read more of *Helpless in Hollywood*! Maybe the president of the United States had figured out how to get away from Spangles O'Leary! But since Mayor Grass hadn't read that far, he didn't have any ideas on how to escape. And besides, this Pimplemuss creature seemed even crazier than Spangles O'Leary. Though Spangles O'Leary was clearly more beautiful, at least the way they described her in the book. Mayor Timothy Grass imagined her to look almost as pretty as Miss Earth.

Pimplemuss came in from the kitchen. "I made you some food," she said. "It's no good starving yourself to death."

Mayor Timothy Grass was hungry. He hadn't eaten anything since the snacks at Grandma Earth's party. And that was what—two, three days ago? He was losing track of time. He could hardly wait for the plate to be set down in front of him.

"I hope you like snarl-hair pasta with sea slug sauce," said Pimplemuss.

The pasta looked like a glop of seaweed. A generous dollop of black goo—like melted tar—was spooned on top of it, and four or five slugs blinked their eyes in a friendly way from the top of the mess. They were brown and pulpy and had little plump arms.

"I can't eat this," said the mayor.

Reebok sniffed the aroma and covered his nose with his paws.

"And why not?" said Pimplemuss in a cross voice. "The sea slugs are fresh as can be. I got them out of our briny vat of homegrown sea slugs."

The slugs waved tiny hands at the mayor to prove how fresh they were.

"I'm a vegetarian," said Mayor Grass, converting on the spot.

"From the planet Vegetar?" said Foomie eagerly. "I had some school friends who came from Vegetar. Tell me, do you know the Pixie family—"

"I'm from Earth," said Mayor Grass, for the ten millionth time. He wanted to weep. "I'm not Santa Claus. I don't live at the North Pole. Vermont only *feels* like the North Pole sometimes. Please. I want to go home. I want to open a can of tomato soup and take a shower and go to sleep. I want to finish reading my book. Don't you know anything about human beings?"

"We're not getting *anywhere* with you!" shouted Pimplemuss. "I make you a perfectly fine meal and you won't even eat it! It's a waste of my time! What do you think I am, your slave?"

"No," said Mayor Grass. "I don't believe in slavery."

"If you don't want it, may *we* eat it?" said Droyd.

"Be my guest. I hope you choke," said Mayor Grass. This was rude of him, but he was feeling beside himself.

"Pimplemuss, may we do a little makeover of the food?" said Peppa.

"Oh, all right, but hurry up," said Pimplemuss. She was striding back and forth with her arms behind her back, thinking. How could she force Santa Claws to show them where his Fortress of Fear was? He was refusing to cooperate.

Droyd and Peppa picked up the plate of snarl-hair pasta with sea slug sauce. They took it to a corner of the starship, to a cubicle that looked to Mayor Grass like a cross between a shower stall and an old-fashioned phone booth. They put the plate of food on the floor. The five slugs all crawled to the top of the slimy pasta and put their little arms around one another for courage. They began to cry. "Sorry," Droyd said to them, "but I hate sea slug sauce."

He looked at Peppa. "What should we make?" he said.

"How about some Santa Claws food?" she said.

"Good idea!" said Droyd.

Mayor Grass watched in surprise. Droyd and Peppa attached a couple of caps to their heads. They looked like ski caps made out of steel wool. The alien called Narr went and flipped the switch. A strange kind of orangey-blue light jittered down from the nozzle in the roof of the chamber. The sea slugs disappeared. The black sauce disappeared. The snarl-hair pasta all stood up straight as if it hadn't been cooked yet, and then *it* disappeared.

In its place there appeared a big pile of oatmeal raisin cookies and a tall, frosty glass of milk.

Mayor Grass's stomach rumbled so loudly that the Fixipuddlings were startled. "Please, may I have some cookies and a sip of milk? Please. I must have something to eat or I'll die!"

"See, this proves you're Santa Claws," said Pimplemuss. "Everyone knows this is the food that Santa Claws eats when he breaks into people's homes and leaves behind his disgusting little time bombs of Numb-All and his midget secret agents. Droyd, Peppa, let him have his meal back. We may be ministers of justice, but we're not cruel."

Peppa fed him the cookies one by one. They were the best cookies Mayor Grass had ever had in his life, better even than any you could buy at Grandma Earth's Baked Goods and Auto Repair Shop. They were chewy and chunky and not too sweet, and the raisins were plump.

Even Reebok ate one and licked Peppa's fingers.

Droyd held the glass so Mayor Grass could sip from it. The milk was full of frothy bubbles. It was cold and wonderful. Vermont cows, try as they might, could never produce milk more delicious. Mayor Grass almost wept at how good it was.

When he was all done, he said, "Did I *really* eat snarl-hair pasta with sea slug sauce?"

"Every bite," said Pimplemuss. "Now look here, Mister Santa Claws. We're getting tired of waiting for you to tell us where your Fortress of Fear is. We're going to have to do something. Our outfits aren't going to last forever." She pulled at the skin on her face as if it were made out of rubber; it snapped back into place with the sound of a fly swatter. "I'm going to have to send a party out to find out what they are saying about your disappearance. No doubt you have your secret agents out looking for you."

Mayor Grass said, "Please, if you'd just untie my hands and let me go, I could explain everything. I'd introduce you to people who will tell you the truth. Doesn't anyone want to know the truth?"

"Not from you, fat boy," said Pimplemuss.

"I resent that," said Mayor Grass. "I admit, in my present outfit I may appear plump. But why won't you untie my hands and let me prove it's a disguise?"

"Look," said Pimplemuss, "we have a mission here. To save this planet from your fiendish ways. Untie you? Hah! We can't even let you go until you tell us where your Fortress of Fear is, so we can liberate all your elfin slaves and declare a new Age of Liberty. And then we have to get our ship fixed so we can head home."

"There are no elfin slaves," said Mayor Grass, sighing. "I tell you, I'm only the simple mayor of a small village on the eastern edge of Vermont! I plow the roads and mow the grass and sell the dog tags and meet with the town selectmen! I make twenty-minute fudge once a year for the bake sale to raise money to hire a lifeguard to protect swimmers! I read library books! I vote! I'm one of the good guys! And I'm not Santa Claus! There is no Santa Claus! I only dress up as Santa Claus on Christmas to cheer the little children! Wherever did you get the idea that there really is a Santa Claus?"

"We have our sources," said Pimplemuss darkly. She didn't want to mention that all their information about him came from the scan-o-matic, which was still broken. "Let me put it this way," she continued. "If you're not Santa Claws, and you're really some beloved creature, how come nobody's come to set you free?"

He couldn't answer that. The same thought had occurred to him. Where were his friends and neighbors? Had anyone noticed he was missing? What about Miss Earth? Didn't she care enough to look for him? Maybe not. He felt discouraged.

But Mayor Grass wasn't ready to give up yet. He

had an idea. Maybe he could trick these creatures into showing him who they really were. "I haven't eaten enough, I'm tired and I'm confused," said Mayor Grass cleverly. "I don't believe you're actually aliens. I think you really *are* elves."

Droyd and Peppa looked proud, like little kids who have fooled their daddy. Droyd said, "Pimplemuss, can we show him?"

"Please, Pimplemuss, please?" said Peppa.

Pimplemuss frowned. "The less you reveal to your enemy, the better," she said.

"Oh, let them have some—what does he call it?—*fun*," said Foomie, who was peering through Foomie's heap of hair, tinkering with the scan-o-matic. "We don't seem to be getting very far in these disguises anyway, do we?"

"Oh, all right then," said Pimplemuss. "Though I still don't know what fun has to do with it. Fun is some weird concept peculiar to Earth. I don't even get the *idea* of fun."

Peppa and Droyd ran back to the particle shower stall. They popped themselves inside and pushed the button for Automatic Reverse. The strange light skittered down around them. Mayor Grass's jaw dropped open. His trick was working—but he almost wished it weren't.

In place of the two elfin children were two small alien creatures. The boy stood on four tentacles, like an oily green octopus on its tiptoes, about a yard high. He had a cluster of small noses, all twitching and some of them running with a pink-ish gunk. There was one eye on the crown of his head, where a man's bald spot might be, and another eye underneath a flap of skin something like a pocket on a boy's shirt. The pocket slid open and the eye winked at Mayor Grass.

The girl looked much the same, only her noses were running with a kind of bluish gunk. So blue for boys and pink for girls *wasn't* a universal law. Mayor Grass had always suspected as much.

"It feels good to be back to normal," said Droyd, tickling Peppa with his fingerpod. Peppa slapped him and he chased her out of the shower stall.

Pimplemuss blinked back a tear. "It's grand to look at you. What they say is right: There's nothing more beautiful than children." The old Fixipud-dling smiled—briefly—at her young companions. "Now get changed back into your disguises. It's time to find out for ourselves where the Fortress of Fear is."

At first Pimplemuss had thought the best idea would be to explore under cover of darkness. But the more she considered this, the less sure she was. After all, the dark was when Santa Claws went abroad in his Reign of Terror. His guards would be on the lookout for him then. Perhaps daylight was safer.

Pimplemuss left Narr and Foomie to guard Reebok and Santa Claws. She and Droyd and

Peppa cautiously let themselves out of the starship. Sunlight hit the snow and bounced back, making the Fixipuddlings squint and shade their eyes with their hands. "Should we go the way we went last time?" said Droyd, pointing toward Foggy Hollow.

"We didn't find the Fortress of Fear that way last time. Let's try our luck the other way," said Pimplemuss.

For a few minutes they walked in silence. The shadows of the trees seemed almost blue on the white world. Small clouds drifted overhead, and a smell of balsam sap eddied in the air. "Earth is somewhat unrefined, for a planet," said Pimplemuss, "but it has a peculiar, rough-hewn beauty all the same, don't you think?"

"I miss the oatmeal-colored skies of home," said Droyd. "I think this blue is disgusting."

"I miss the green sunrises over Mount Monotony," said Peppa.

"So do I," said Pimplemuss. "But this is so exotic. A warm yellow sun, a blue sky, cold powdery snow. You'll remember this your whole lives and tell your grandchildren."

"If we ever get home and *have* grandchildren," said Droyd.

"If we can't have grandchildren, can we have a dog?" said Peppa. "There's never anything to *do* in the starship! Only homework and chores and meals and bedtime! That's why we were driving the starship when it crashed. We were *bored*."

"If you're going to amuse yourselves by crashing our starship, I think *you* need a dose of Numb-All," said Pimplemuss.

"But what do other creatures in the universe do for *fun?*" said Droyd.

"Lois has a pet. We want one too," said Peppa firmly.

"That *fun* thing again. Give it a rest. First things first," said Pimplemuss. "Find out where the Fortress of Fear is, liberate the slaves, and then worry about getting our starship fixed. We'll be home within a hundred years; it'll go by like that. You won't notice that you're not having any fun. We'll do our times tables. Our spelling bees. Maybe we can practice penmanship, too."

Droyd sighed. Peppa sighed.

They came to a wooden building. A sign in front said:

THE VERMONT MUSEUM
OF INTERESTING FACTS
TO KNOW AND TELL

They peeped in the windows, but they couldn't see any two-headed chickens in the gloom.

"What a shame," said Droyd. "We could have strapped our WordSearch dials, one on each neck, and listened to the heads argue with each other."

"Look," said Peppa, "the door's unlocked!"

Sure enough, the door opened at their push.

Pimplemuss found a light switch and they all read a handwritten sign that said, *Hi there! Enjoy the Museum! Please leave a donation in the coffee can on the radiator, and turn off the lights when you leave. Mayor Timothy Grass.*

The museum was one big room. Pimplemuss, Droyd, and Peppa wandered around in amazement, staring at the exhibits. Glass cases against the walls showed impressive treasures. Signs nearby explained what they were. A bird's nest made all out of lace *(Built by a Robin Who Lived Above Betty's Bridal Barn)*. A piece of fieldstone that had eroded over the eons to resemble President Lyndon Johnson. And there was the famous two-headed chicken from Puster Center! One head looked as if it wanted to speak, and the other head looked as if it had heard enough already.

"Look at this!" shouted Droyd. "Here's a display showing how a disgusting thing called a caterpillar becomes a butterfly! Isn't *that* an interesting fact to know and tell!"

"It's not so unusual," said Pimplemuss. "After all, when you young things grow up, you'll shed your lower tentacles and develop legs and feathers like other adult Fixipuddlings. It's the way of nature all over the universe, I guess: Grow and change."

"We should have a museum like this on Fixipuddle," said Peppa.

Pimplemuss was getting impatient. "Let's go. Anybody have a donation to leave?"

They didn't know what a donation was, but Droyd ran outside and got some snow and left it in the coffee can on the radiator. Maybe that would do. Then they turned off the lights and closed the door behind them.

They wandered around some more. Once they heard a ferocious rumble, and they all jumped into the bracken at the side of the road. A long yellow vehicle on big black wheels came jouncing along. It was filled with creatures—screaming elves? "They've captured some more," said Pimplemuss. "Quick! Follow that conveyance!"

They chased it along, but it quickly outpaced them. Still, they felt they were on the right track. Another twenty minutes and they saw where the yellow thing had parked—in front of a low brick building. A sign out front said:

THE JOSIAH FAWCETT ELEMENTARY SCHOOL
HAMLET, VERMONT

They crept up to the nearest window. It just happened to be the window that looked in on Miss Earth's class.

16

The Common Sense
of Miss Earth

Miss Earth stood at the front of the room. "I know you are all disappointed to be back to school so soon after Christmas," she said. "But it can't be helped. We had so many snow days in mid-December. If we don't make up the time now, we'll be in school until mid-July. And nobody wants *that*. But we can leave the room decorated for a while; it lends a pleasant atmosphere, don't you think?"

"It'll lend a pleasant atmosphere when you finish reading *A Christmas Carol* to us," said Salim, holding the book.

"Later, Salim. First I must take attendance."

Miss Earth bent her head over her notebook. No one was looking at the window to see the eyebrows and noses of three elves appear over the windowsill.

Miss Earth read the names. "Salim Bannerjee. Nina Bueno. Moshe Cohn. Carly Garfunkel. Sammy Grubb. Pearl Hotchkiss. Lois Kennedy the Third.

Anna Maria Mastrangelo. Forest Eugene Mopp. Thekla Mustard. Fawn Petros. Mike Saint Michael. Stan Tomaski. Sharday Wren. Hector Yellow."

Fifteen childish voices said, "Here, Miss Earth," one after the other.

Miss Earth slammed her attendance book shut. "You know," she said, "sometimes I wish you could call me Miss Germaine instead of Miss Earth."

"But we like 'Miss Earth,' Miss Earth," said her students.

"But Miss Earth makes me sound like a contestant in a beauty pageant," said their teacher.

"You could win as Miss Earth!" cried Salim Bannerjee. "You could easily beat out Miss Venus! Or Miss Mars!"

"Well, I should hope so," said Miss Earth. "I don't believe I look like a Martian."

"You could win as Miss Solar System," said Sammy Grubb.

"You could win as Miss Galaxy," added Thekla Mustard.

"You could win as Miss Milky Way!" inserted Lois Kennedy the Third, trying to keep her profile high among the Tattletales in case a surprise election was coming anytime soon.

"You could win as Miss Universe!" said Pearl Hotchkiss, back from Connecticut.

"You could win," said Moshe Cohn, who always read the science section in the Tuesday *New York Times* when it came in the mail the following

Friday, "as Miss Ultimate Reality in the Space-Time Continuum!"

"Surely you exaggerate my virtues," said Miss Earth, blushing, but she was pleased. She was a hard-working teacher, and she liked to be appreciated. "Well, you may call me what you like as long as you don't call me late for supper!" She was quick with a quip, too.

Her kids had all heard that joke before, but they laughed respectfully.

Outside the classroom, Pimplemuss was about to have an attack of rage. Droyd and Peppa, who knew the symptoms well, were sitting on her. Peppa stuffed Pimplemuss's mouth full of snow. Droyd held her hands down so she couldn't fight back. Pimplemuss struggled hard and got madder and madder. Finally she blew her cover—literally. The disguise as a cute old grandmother elf began to dissolve in a glowing pattern of blue and orange light.

Droyd and Peppa dragged Pimplemuss away, past a wire fence and a snow-covered jungle gym, and into some woods. There, at last, Pimplemuss's true looks reasserted themselves. She stood nine feet tall, white and feathery. Her pupils rotated like half a dozen lazy eyes.

"The nerve of those twerps!" she cried. "That Miss Earth thing a beauty? Don't they know true beauty when they see it? Miss Earth isn't fit to sell snacks at an intergalactic beauty pageant! Those little creeps don't know what they're talking about!"

"Oh, Pimplemuss," said Droyd, "you're the fairest of them all."

"Not just *fair*," shouted Pimplemuss, "drop-dead gorgeous!"

"Also patient and kind," said Peppa, stretching the truth a bit. "Now, Pimplemuss, we know we wanted to find out where the Fortress of Fear was. But we better get you back to the starship *Loiterbug*. We don't want anyone seeing you like this or we'll be found out. We'll have to try again later."

"That Miss Earth. She's not even pretty!" stewed Pimplemuss. "That hair the color of sunlight! Those big coppery-brown eyes! That bumpy figure! Curvy here, slender there—it's so—*undecided*! I've seen sea slugs in my sauce who look better than she does!"

"Of course you have, we all have," said Droyd. "Now come on, before we get in trouble." The young Fixipuddlings, dragging Pimplemuss by her downy white limbs, hurried back to the starship. Mayor Grass and Reebok saw Pimplemuss in her true form, looking like a giant enraged snowy-white three-legged goose with eyes in her neck and chest. Mayor Grass and Reebok immediately fainted.

"See," said Droyd kindly, "they fainted at your beauty."

"As they should," said Pimplemuss. She took to her room in a huff. Her friends could hear the sound of shattering glass, as little jars of beauty ointment went crashing against the metal walls.

But back at the Josiah Fawcett Elementary School, the conversation had turned to serious matters.

"Now, my little grape-pickers in the vineyards of truth," said Miss Earth, "I hope you had a fine Christmas and Hanukkah."

"Vacation was too brief," said Sammy Grubb, "but who could be in the mood for vacation? It's all been too alarming."

"I assume you mean the disappearance of our dear mayor," said Miss Earth.

"*What?*" said Pearl Hotchkiss. She hadn't heard about this because she'd been away.

"There are some theories circulating," said Sammy Grubb.

"And what might these theories be?" said Miss Earth.

Thekla stood. "The Tattletales believe that the mayor has been a victim of accidental time travel. He has been whisked out of the present day into the past or the future. We're not sure which."

"Very interesting," said Miss Earth. "And why do you think that?"

"It only makes sense," said Thekla. "He was dressed as Santa Claus when he disappeared. Maybe some poor soul like Ebenezer Scrooge needed a lesson in life, and Mayor Grass was selected to do the job. The only questions we have are these: How do we find him? How do we get him back?"

"It's a puzzle," agreed Miss Earth. "I don't know much about time travel. You'll have to go to the library and ask Mr. Dewey for a book about it."

"There's another theory," said Sammy Grubb, leaping to his feet. "I think that Mayor Grass was abducted by Bigfoot."

"And why do you think that?" said Miss Earth.

"It stands to reason," said Sammy Grubb. "Bigfoot usually stays way up north because he likes snow and cold. But I bet this year he's been able to venture farther and farther south because it's been so cold and snowy. Bigfoot may have come across Mayor Grass on Christmas Eve and smelled cookies in his pocket."

"Oh dear," said Miss Earth. "I think the notion of Bigfoot is farfetched, Sammy. But Mayor Grass did have some cookies in his pocket—some gingerbread men. So assuming it was Bigfoot, or some other creature afflicted with gigantism, where did he or she take Mayor Grass?"

Sammy Grubb didn't want to say the part of the theory in which Mayor Grass was eaten alive. It didn't seem polite. "Maybe he took Mayor Grass to his home in the frozen north," said Sammy Grubb.

"But why?" said Miss Earth.

"To bake him *cookies?*" snorted Thekla Mustard.

"Hey, what can I say?" said Sammy Grubb. "It's just a theory. It's better than your dumb theory. What makes your theory so great? Just who exactly whisked Mayor Grass away to serve as the Ghost of

Christmas Here, There, and Everywhere, anyway?"

"Bigfoot," said Thekla Mustard. "Or should I say Big Mouth?"

Pearl Hotchkiss raised her hand. "Pearl," said Miss Earth, "you're always a voice of sweet reason in the fray. What do you think?"

"I'm so frightened to hear about this," said Pearl. "Do you think Mayor Grass got hit in the head and has amnesia? Maybe he's wandering around in the woods without any idea who he is."

"What hit him in the head?" said Miss Earth.

"Bigfoot hit him with a snowball!" cried Thekla mockingly. The Tattletales, even Lois Kennedy the Third, giggled in support of their Empress.

"No, Ebenezer Scrooge hit him with a copy of *A Christmas Carol*!" hooted Sammy Grubb. The Copycats all chortled loyally.

"Maybe something more ordinary. Maybe some snow fell off a tree limb," said Pearl. "Who knows? It could happen. Shouldn't somebody alert the FBI?"

"My mother called them," said Miss Earth. "They said Mayor Grass couldn't qualify for being a missing person until he'd been gone a week. They thought he probably was taking a little unscheduled vacation time, and that we were being nervous for nothing. Now, my little theorists, let's take our minds off our worries. It's time for me to continue in *A Christmas Carol*. I promised Salim."

"Miss Earth?" said Pearl Hotchkiss. She wanted

Sammy Grubb to know that she didn't *entirely* overlook his suggestion, even if it was ridiculous. After all, she wanted to keep on Sammy's good side. And who knew? Boys could be right sometimes. "Just one question," said Pearl. "Bigfoot might be the culprit. But what about the Abominable Snowman? Or are they the same thing?"

No one in the room could answer the question. Miss Earth gave Moshe Cohn permission to run to the school library and look it up in the *Whole Earth Encyclopedia*.

Then Miss Earth opened up the book and read some more from *A Christmas Carol*. The children sat in rapt attention, especially Salim. With his chin in his hands, he listened to how the terrible Ghost of Christmas Yet To Come appeared. The Ghost warned of the possible death of the poor little child, Tiny Tim. The Ghost showed Scrooge his own tombstone reading EBENEZER SCROOGE. Scrooge begged for mercy. "I will honour Christmas in my heart, and try to keep it all the year. I will live in the Past, the Present, and the Future. The Spirits of all Three shall strive within me. I will not shut out the lessons that they teach. Oh, tell me I may sponge away the writing on this stone!"

A sob caught in Miss Earth's throat. All the children looked at the floor. They were all thinking the same thing: One day soon there might need to be a tombstone for Timothy Grass, mayor of Hamlet, lost from this life on Christmas Eve.

17

A Spy in Their Midst

Pimplemuss came out of the particle shower stall. Once again she looked like a gentle old elf, with cheeks red as candy apples and lots of wrinkles wreathing her warm eyes. "Well," she said, "that whole stupid expedition was a great big waste of time, thank you very much."

"You shouldn't have lost your temper," said Peppa. "It's never a good idea."

"Don't lecture me or I'll put you in the particle shower and turn you into a meatloaf."

Reebok flared his nostrils at the sound of a word he loved.

"Now wait a minute," said Mayor Grass. "Look, the milk and cookies have helped me come to my senses. It's time to be straight with one another. Who are you really?"

"Who gave you permission to ask questions?" said Foomie. "Really, you're getting tiresome."

"Where did you come from? What do you want?" said Mayor Grass. Were these the advance guard of an invading army? If so, it was his job to stop them. After all, he was the mayor.

"We told you already, we hail from the great planet of Fixipuddle," said Pimplemuss. "We've been on a journey through the galaxy to find an oppressed planet to liberate. It's for my merit badge. Now don't bother us, chunky man. We have plans to make." She sat down with the others.

Mayor Grass felt more hopeless than ever. If he hadn't fully believed they were aliens until he saw them change before his eyes, no wonder they didn't believe he was a simple mayor, not Santa Claus. With his hands tied, though, he couldn't pull off his fake beard or remove the pillow from his stomach. And they wouldn't listen to him when he tried to explain. So, since there was nothing else to do, he listened to them. And his spirits sank even deeper.

"I don't know if I trust myself out there," Pimplemuss said. "I haven't done very well so far. Look how I lost my temper—and I'm usually so calm and collected."

"Indeed," said Foomie, lying through Foomie's teeth. The others all nodded dolefully.

"I think we need a secret agent to go places we can't go," said Pimplemuss. "And there's one of us who will be especially good and fit right in without alarming anyone."

"Who? Who?" said Droyd and Peppa, wriggling importantly in their seats.

Pimplemuss turned and said, "Here, boy. Here, boy!" Reebok got up and shuffled over to her. "Who's the good little doggie then?" said Pimplemuss. "Who's the best little spy around? Who is it? Yes, it's *you!*" Reebok wagged his tail and almost broke his spine trying to lick Pimplemuss's face.

"Reebok! Have you no loyalty?" cried Mayor Grass.

"We want you to go out there and listen to their plans," said Pimplemuss. She chucked Reebok under the chin, then scratched him behind the ears. "Find out where the Fortress of Fear is. Find out if they're on our trail. That's a nice dog. Good dog! You'll get a snack if you're well behaved." Reebok was in an ecstasy of love for Pimplemuss. He pawed her white dress with the red and green piping, making dog footprints on her bib. "Just stay out of sight," said Pimplemuss. "Can you handle that, Reebok? Food is food. Come back here where we feed you the best. Understand?"

Reebok looked uncertain, and he barked several times.

"Oh, you want the menu?" said Pimplemuss. "Okay. I'm going to prepare a big treat for you. Narr?" The old elf with the fluttering beard came forward. "Narr, give me your WordSearch dial. You're not going to need it for a while."

Narr obliged.

"Now go into the particle shower stall, if you don't mind."

Narr obliged again, but hesitantly.

Pimplemuss said to Narr, "This is all for a good cause, old friend. I need a sufficient mass of live organic matter to pull off creating a really convincing pile of food. Don't worry. I won't leave you like this." Narr looked alarmed, but since he didn't speak, he couldn't protest. Pimplemuss jammed the wire mesh cap on her head and spun a few dials. Then she jabbed the on switch.

The blue and orange light crackled down out of the light spout. In an instant, the old elf with the long white beard had disappeared.

In Narr's place was a huge dish. It was piled high with food that Pimplemuss guessed would appeal to a dog. There was a sirloin of beef, charred and chewy; there were meatballs and sausages. The whole mound of deliciousness stood about three feet high.

Except for an oatmeal cookie, Reebok hadn't eaten in three days. "Ruff!" he shouted. Tears of joy streamed from his eyes.

"When you're done," said Pimplemuss. "Are you ready to go and spy for us?"

"Ruff!" barked Reebok.

"And what are you especially to look out for?" said Pimplemuss.

"Ruff!" roared Reebok.

"Exactly," said Pimplemuss. "Go, my spy, and learn what you can of the Fortress of Fear. We have to know if Santa Claws's private army is preparing to make an attack against us."

"Ruff!" growled Reebok. Pimplemuss threw the door open and, like a rocket, out shot Reebok.

"You can't *do* this to Narr," shouted Mayor Grass. "It's inhuman!"

"Perhaps you have forgotten," said Pimplemuss coldly, "we have never claimed to *be* human. We wouldn't know how."

But Droyd and Peppa thought that Pimplemuss had gone too far, too. What used to be Narr quivered in the dish, smelling of garlic and oregano and rich beef gravy. Foomie said, "Really, Pimplemuss, aren't we getting a little carried away here?"

But Pimplemuss only said, "Don't you all second-guess me! I'm the commander and you're the crew, and you'll all serve me as pies and puddings if I require it!" Then she stormed off to her room and slammed the door.

"She's quite the handful," said Mayor Grass.

Foomie, Peppa, and Droyd nodded. They didn't know whether to be proud of her or ashamed of her. From the dish, Narr steamed in a slightly delicious way. Against his own best wishes, Mayor Grass heard his stomach rumbling.

"What do we do now?" said Peppa.

Droyd shrugged his shoulders.

Mayor Grass looked down on them. He knew they were his kidnappers, and that perhaps they meant him harm. But still, they were only young ones. He felt sorry for them. Well, this was why he was a good mayor; he cared about everyone. Even the children of invading aliens.

He remembered Salim and his interest in *A Christmas Carol.* Salim was an alien, too, only a different kind. "Do you want to hear a story?" said Mayor Grass.

"What's that?" said Peppa.

"I could tell you a story."

"What do you mean?" said Droyd. "What's a story?"

If they didn't know what fun was, it made sense they didn't know what a story was either. "Well," said Mayor Grass, remembering how hungry he was to get back to *Helpless in Hollywood.* "Stories are what you tell each other to pass the time and to amuse yourselves. Stories help you figure out how to be human."

"I thought WordSearch dials did that."

Foomie looked a bit suspicious. Mayor Grass thought Foomie might alert Pimplemuss that something dangerous was going on. Mayor Grass pretended to be bored with the conversation. He whistled a minute and glanced at the ceiling, and after a while he said, in a conversational voice, "Once upon a time, did you know, there was a terrible vicious bad-tempered old creature—"

"—named Santa Claws!" said Peppa.

"—named Pimplemuss," muttered Droyd.

"—named Ebenezer Scrooge," said Mayor Grass. "He was a rich old man, and mighty, but he hated music, beauty, and mirth. Now one day—and it happened to be the day before Christmas—he was in his study counting his money . . ."

*

Reebok was a dog with a mission. Once away from the starship, he remembered the old familiar smells of the world. How entrancing! A badger had eaten something moldy and had become ill—what a delightful smell! A deer family had come along and made their beds for the night beneath these trees—how appealing! Reebok almost forgot his instructions.

But then he remembered. He charged along Squished Toad Road, following his nose. He was looking for Lois. Lois would know what was going on. Lois was the Human Being of Life—of Reebok's life, anyway. If he had had a vote, Reebok would always have voted for Lois for Empress. But Reebok wasn't a Tattletale. He was a dog, and Lois was his Big Adorableness.

His nose said here, his nose said there. Reebok found himself on the grounds of the Josiah Fawcett Elementary School. He was too small to jump up onto the window ledge of Miss Earth's classroom, so he waited behind a bush near the front door.

Before long a mother came out, dragging a little kid who had to go to the dentist due to too many candy canes.

Reebok slipped into the school before the door could swing shut again.

He pattered down the hallway. He almost bumped into a kindergartner, who looked down and said, "Nice kitty!" and tried to pet him with sticky hands. But Reebok hurried along. At a certain point he smelled the lunch from the school cafeteria and almost went to investigate. But though he was hungry, the school lunch didn't smell enough like food to attract him. So he continued along the hall until he got to the door of Miss Earth's classroom.

There were lots of coats on hooks in the hallway. Reebok nipped at a couple until he was able to drag one down. He slipped under it. Great hiding place! Then he inched forward. The door was open. He could hear voices.

✳

Inside the room, Moshe Cohn was saying, "Actually, the *Whole Earth Encyclopedia* says that Bigfoot and the Abominable Snowman may be based on the same idea, but they're not exactly the same thing. Bigfoot is a creature in Native American lore. The Abominable Snowman is from Europe. Bigfoot is sometimes called Sasquatch. Bigfoot is more often brown and twiggy, like a

116

beast made out of the forest. The Abominable Snowman has icy-white fur. That's all I know."

"You did a wonderful job," said Miss Earth. "Does anyone have anything to add?"

"I say, whatever it is, we call it Bigfoot," said Sammy Grubb. "The word *abominable* is too hard to say. Besides, *abominable* means 'hateful,' right? Deserving of being hated?"

"That's correct," said Miss Earth.

"But we don't know if this creature is hateful. So I think that's an insult to a creature we haven't even seen with our own eyes yet."

"Very well, then. That's kind and thoughtful of you, Sammy," said Miss Earth. "We will call the character Bigfoot unless we learn otherwise. I don't think there's anything to suggest that Bigfoot actually carried Mayor Grass away, but I'm willing to try to keep an open mind. Stranger things have happened. There is the matter of the Santa Claus cap that Lois found near Foggy Hollow."

"And the voice I heard in Foggy Hollow. Don't forget that!" said Sammy Grubb.

"Of course," said Thekla Mustard, "I believe that Mayor Grass has slipped into a time warp and is even now treading up and down the streets of Hamlet, Vermont, some two hundred years ago."

"Hamlet wasn't even settled two hundred years ago," said Miss Earth.

"Then he'd be especially lost and lonely, wouldn't he?" said Thekla Mustard. At which point Reebok

117

smelled a salt tear from the efficient tear ducts of Miss Earth.

"Personally, I think this is ridiculous," said Pearl Hotchkiss. She hadn't wanted to contradict Sammy Grubb because she liked him so much, but, in the end, common sense was common sense. "Next someone will be saying he's been abducted by aliens from outer space. I mean, *really!*"

"Now, Pearl," said Miss Earth. "It's unlikely Mayor Grass has become the Ghost of Christmas Past, Present, or To Come. It's unlikely he's been kidnapped by Bigfoot, either. As for abduction by space aliens, I tend to agree with you: fat chance. However, if it meant our going out to meet aliens and beg for Tim Grass's release, we would do it. In life, you must do what you must, however silly it may seem. Don't you all agree?"

"Yes, Miss Earth," said Pearl.

"Yes, Miss Earth," said Pearl's classmates.

"Yes, Miss Earth," said Miss Earth, agreeing with herself.

Reebok thought he had heard enough. He didn't rush in and have a joyous reunion with Lois. He had another idea. He turned and raced away.

18

Reebok's Report

When Reebok returned to the starship *Loiterbug*, he flung himself into Pimplemuss's lap. The Fixipuddling caressed him and scratched behind his ears. But she kept her head angled so she could hear Mayor Grass.

"So what did Ebenezer Scrooge do then? Once the Ghost of Christmas Past left him? Keep going! Tell us!" she cried.

But Mayor Grass was too disappointed to continue. "You turncoat," he said to Reebok. "You little doggie Benedict Arnold. You traitor. You had a chance to bring help and you blew it."

"Ruff," said Reebok.

"Very rough," said Mayor Grass. Still, he was grateful for a break. Telling the Fixipuddlings the story of *A Christmas Carol* was keeping their minds off harming him, or anyone else. But it was hard work to remember the whole story. Some of it was sounding a lot like *Helpless in Hollywood*. However, since the Fixipuddlings didn't seem to know about stories, he wasn't worried that they would notice.

Pimplemuss was holding Reebok back from the heap of baked meats and doggie treats that was really Narr. "Not yet, my little four-legged spy," she said. "First you must tell me what you know." Mayor Grass thought he could see the pile of food tremble. Narr was afraid he would really get eaten by the hungry pooch.

"Sit," said Pimplemuss. "Sit."

Out of habit, Droyd, Peppa, and Foomie all sat. Narr was already sitting, in a manner of speaking. Reebok ran around in anticipation, staring at the Narr-meal.

"I said," said Pimplemuss, "SIT DOWN."

Reebok sat.

"That's a good boy," said Pimplemuss. She picked up the WordSearch dial that she had removed from around Narr. She strapped it onto Reebok. Then she adjusted a few knobs. "There now. All right, boy. Tell me what you know."

"Ruff," said Reebok.

"I beg your pardon?" said Pimplemuss.

"Ruff," he repeated. "Ruff ruff."

"Whatever do you mean?"

"I mean," said Reebok, "it's rough to have to make conversation when there's a plate of dinner as high as a mailbox standing eight feet away!"

Pimplemuss said, "Foomie, darling, draw the

drape so that our secret agent won't get distracted by what's on the menu."

"I can't believe this!" shouted Mayor Grass. "Reebok, you can talk?"

"More than that," said Reebok, himself surprised. "I can sing, too. Would anyone like to hear a little something jazzy? Be-bop, be-diddle-diddle—"

"No, we would not," said Pimplemuss. "Listen up. You tell me what they're planning, and you'll have the supper of your dreams."

"It's hard to know where to start," said Reebok.

"Start at the beginning," said Pimplemuss.

"Good idea," said Reebok. He ground his hindquarters into the floor and affected a dignified expression. He cleared his throat. "Unaccustomed as I am to public speaking," he started.

"Skip the rhetoric and get to the report," snarled Pimplemuss.

"I learned what they think happened to Old Fatso over there."

"Reebok!" shouted Mayor Grass. "How rude!"

"There are two theories," said Reebok. He lowered his chin onto his front paws and appeared to concentrate. "Some think that a ghost came and took him to the future or the past. Some think a ferocious monster called Bigfoot carried him away. Do I smell a pork chop somewhere?"

"Well, those theories are near enough." Pimplemuss chuckled. "As far as this planet knows, we *did* come out of the future or the past. It's so hard to keep an accurate calendar when you're skipping across time thresholds the way we do. How about this snow monster? What's it supposed to look like?"

"About nine feet tall," said Reebok, "comes in two attractive designer colors, either brown or white."

"I can look like a Bigfoot," said Pimplemuss. "Convenient. Now, Reebok, pay attention. Did you find out where the Fortress of Fear was?"

"Yes, I did," said Reebok.

Mayor Grass's jaw dropped open. "You don't know what you're saying!" he cried.

"Sorry," said Reebok. "I haven't eaten in three days, and that pile of food is looking pretty good to me."

"Well, where is the Fortress of Fear?" said Pimplemuss. "Is it nearby?"

"Very nearby," said Reebok. "Do you remember you told us you lost your cool and became your true self? And a very beautiful self you are, I might add, something like a cross between a nine-foot three-legged white bear and a duck with an eye disorder."

"Thank you," cooed Pimplemuss, fiddling with her braids. "I can't wait to get back to my true beauty."

"Do you remember where you were when that disguise meltdown happened?" asked Reebok.

"Yes, I remember that place. It was called the

Josiah Fawcett Elementary School. What about it?"

"You stumbled on the Fortress of Fear," said Reebok. "Anyone have a pound of luncheon meat in a side pocket somewhere? Hmmmm?"

"But that didn't look anything like the Fortress of Fear we saw in the news bulletin!" cried Pimplemuss.

"Of course not," snapped Reebok. "Do you think they'd broadcast what it *really* looks like? So any brave soul wishing to overthrow the dictator would know exactly where to go? No, the Fortress of Fear is cleverly disguised on the outside as a grade school. But if you go there tomorrow, you'll surely be able to free the elves!"

"What nonsense!" shouted Mayor Grass.

"Why not today?" said Pimplemuss. "Why not right now? I can't wait!"

"Because," said Reebok, who had a plan in mind, "the elves are very fragile at night. Any little excitement, like the possibility of liberation, and they would go all to pieces. Literally. Little bits of elf flesh flying all over the room. Disgusting. Tomorrow morning would be much safer for them. And also much more hygienic for you, as well as more gratifying."

Mayor Grass sobbed. "I can't believe what you're saying!"

"You've done well," said Pimplemuss.

"Now do I get to eat my dinner?" said Reebok. His nose was twitching.

"You sure do deserve it," said Pimplemuss. "But not Narr. Let me cook you up some snarl-hair pasta in sea slug sauce."

"Just one thing," said Reebok. "I have to go outside for a moment."

"What for?" said Pimplemuss.

"I have to do something personal."

"What thing?"

"That thing dogs do. You know. Near a hydrant if you're lucky?"

"I think he means a Private Moment," said Foomie.

"Oh," said Pimplemuss. "Well, okay. Will you be long?"

"A little while. But I'll be back."

Pimplemuss opened the door. Reebok shot out as if he had to do something personal *very* urgently. But in a moment he was lost from view.

19

The Fortress of Fear

However much Lois disliked Thekla Mustard, she had to give her credit. Thekla was a great organizer. Not for nothing did she get voted Empress of the Tattletales *every time*. Thekla Mustard had verve, snap, and follow-through.

And in Thekla's own way, she was kind of kind. When the news that Reebok was also missing had gotten around, Thekla organized the Tattletales into search parties every afternoon. Even Pearl Hotchkiss came and helped. They met at Lois's house, and all held hands to commune with the spirit of Reebok. (More than once Lois was on the edge of tears, but she held back. Future leaders of the Tattletales didn't cry. It wasn't seemly.)

Then the Tattletales had broken into groups of two or three and wandered around the village, waving links of breakfast sausage and calling, "Here, Reebok! Come and get it, boy!" Sometimes the

Tattletales ran into the Copycats, who were combing the same neighborhood looking for evidence of Bigfoot.

"Find any hairy footprints in the snow, Sammy?" said Thekla once when she met her arch-rival by the monument in Ethan Allen Park.

"Not yet, but we will," said Sammy Grubb.

"I wonder," said Thekla. "Could it be that there are no footprints in the snow because the Ghost of Christmas Past, Present, or Future doesn't *leave* footprints?"

"How do you know ghosts don't leave footprints?" said Sammy Grubb.

Thekla didn't even bother to answer. It was so obvious. Ghosts had hands and heads and bodies, but they trailed off into wisps at the bottom, like the tag ends of speech bubbles in the Sunday comics. Everybody knew that.

Pearl and the Tattletales were back at Lois's house, putting the sausages in the Kennedys' freezer for another day, when Lois heard a noise outside. She whipped her head around.

"Reebok!" she cried.

The Tattletales and Pearl looked at one another with joy. What a frantic sound of barking! The girls crowded around the back door, which Lois threw open. Reebok soared through the air like a circus beagle shooting out of a cannon. He knocked Lois over and licked her face as if she were made of breakfast sausages.

"Reebok!" cried Lois, over and over. "My own Reebok! Where have you been, boy?"

Reebok paused in his frantic kissing. He panted for a minute with his tongue hanging out of his mouth. Then he said, "Honey, you're never going to believe this."

The girls froze. Lois's eyebrows shot up. "Did you say something?" she said.

"As a matter of public record," said Reebok, "the answer is yes. I did speak. Surprise, surprise."

Lois looked around. Her mother was ironing while watching a soap opera on TV. Her baby brother was hitting the new rocking horse with a plastic baseball bat, saying "Bad Bigfoot! Bad Bigfoot!"

"Upstairs," hissed Reebok. "I don't have time to be a celebrity. We have work to do. By the way, do I smell a little hint of hamburger in the air?"

Lois grabbed some dog biscuits from the kitchen, and then the dog and the seven Tattletales and Pearl Hotchkiss clattered up the stairs. Lois's mother didn't tell them to stop running in the house because she was crying over the soaps. The commercial came on—"More doctors recommend Numb-All for fast relief of muscular pain!"—and only then did Mrs. Kennedy call out, "You sound like a herd of buffalo gals! Try not to crash through the floorboards, please!"

The Tattletales didn't listen. Reebok was telling his story.

"They've got Mayor Grass," he said, "and their leader, an old woman named Pimplemuss, is a duck! A huge duck on three legs. The one called Narr is a stack of roasted meats on a plate. There are two kids, named Droyd and Peppa. Also a big talking clot of hairball, they call it Foomie. It looks like an English sheepdog getting an electric shock, all frizz and no face. Is there any leftover porterhouse steak going lonely?"

"I don't understand," said Lois. "Reebok, slow down! Who has Mayor Grass? Is it the Ghosts of Christmas Past, Present, and Future?"

"There are five of them," yapped Reebok.

"Five of who?" asked Thekla sharply. "Five abominable snow monsters? Five Bigfoots—I mean Bigfeet?"

"I need a drink of water," panted Reebok. "I'm talking *alien elves*. Alien elves! Can you believe it?" He ran into the bathroom to take a drink out of the toilet, but the lid was down. Lois hurried to put some water in the soup bowl she kept on her radiator for when the winter air got too dry.

"Did he say elves? Or Elvis? Alien Elvis?" said Thekla. "My gracious, this is worse than I thought! I know some folks think Elvis Presley is still alive, but has he become an alien?"

"You ain't nothing but a hound dog," sang Carly Garfunkel. Everyone gave her a dirty look, especially Reebok. Carly fell silent.

"I didn't say Alien Elvis," said Reebok, once his

thirst was slaked. "I said *elves*. Like Christmas elves. You know, pointy shoes and striped leggings, shorts with big buttons, funny hats with feathers in them. The whole nine yards."

"Mayor Grass has been kidnapped by alien hooligans?" shouted Thekla.

"The very same," said Reebok grimly, "from outer space."

"Yikes," said Pearl Hotchkiss. "Boy, is Sammy going to be disappointed it's not Bigfoot. Maybe I should go tell him."

"But how can you talk?" said Nina Bueno to Reebok.

"Something to do with this fanny pack I'm wearing," said Reebok, "but don't ask me. Now look, we don't have much time. We've got to gather our forces in order to prepare for an invasion of elves tomorrow morning!"

"This is too important to do alone," said Thekla Mustard. "Reebok, we'd better tell my parents."

"We *don't have time*," said Reebok. "Besides, I won't talk in front of your parents, so they won't believe you. If they did, they'd make a big mistake. They'd try to storm the space ship and get Mayor Grass, and that would be real trouble. Those elves can turn you into mincemeat just by putting on a shower cap and thinking meaty thoughts. No siree bob. We have a good chance of negotiating for the Mayor's release if we play our cards right."

"We should tell someone," said Pearl Hotchkiss.

"We should tell Miss Earth. She'll bring a cool head and a dedicated heart to any effort."

"And we may have to get the help of the Copycats, too," said Reebok.

"We hate to work with the Copycats," said Thekla Mustard.

"Thekla," said Lois Kennedy the Third. "Get a grip. This is Mayor Grass's life we're talking about."

Thekla blinked twice. The Empress of the Tattletales didn't like being scolded by one of her subjects. But one sign of a good leader is the ability to take correction. "You're right, Lois," she said. "Good point."

Thekla so rarely complimented Lois that Lois gaped.

Thekla plowed on. "For Mayor Grass, we'll do it. Lois, go see if you can get Sammy Grubb on the phone. Tell him to get his guys together and meet us at Grandma Earth's Baked Goods and Auto Repair Shop in an hour."

Lois didn't like being told what to do by Thekla, especially in her own home. But Mayor Grass's safety was more important than her own sense of pride. As she got up to make the phone calls, she heard Thekla say, "What are we going to do, Reebok?"

"I don't know," said Reebok. "I've done everything I could. I'm a dog. My ideas are all doggie ideas. You'd better come up with some human ideas."

"I'd better go have a high-level powwow with

Sammy Grubb," said Thekla. She glanced around. "Lois, get your spy coat. Come along. I may need a *chargé d'affaires.* We better figure out a plan quickly, or all is lost."

"What about me?" said Pearl Hotchkiss, a little huffily. "I want to tell Sammy the news. After all, I'm the voice of sweet reason in the fray. Miss Earth says so all the time."

"That may be," said Thekla Mustard, "but you're not a Tattletale. And you don't have a neat coat like Lois. Never underestimate the value of the proper accessories, Pearl."

Thekla Mustard and Lois Kennedy the Third, accompanied by Reebok, hurried to meet Sammy Grubb by the newspaper rack in the Grand Union. Sammy showed up with Salim Bannerjee. Sammy had appointed Salim his emergency factotum for the afternoon.

Reebok didn't want to be seen talking in the Grand Union. "I'll be all over the front page of the *National Town Crier,*" he said. He suggested that Lois and Thekla fill Sammy and Salim in on the details.

". . . so you see," said Thekla, "it wasn't the Ghost of Christmas Past, Present, or To Come, nor was it Bigfoot."

"Well, who could have guessed it would be aliens?" said Sammy.

"If I remember correctly," said Thekla, "to be honest, Pearl Hotchkiss did."

"Hey, look," said Salim. The headlines of the *National Town Crier* screamed in thirty-point type, UFO SIGHTINGS ON CHRISTMAS EVE! There was a photo of an alien who looked a little bit like E.T. after a makeover.

"That's so phony," said Sammy Grubb. "He looks more plastic than a Baby Wet'n'Dry. Nobody could believe this stuff."

They talked about possible strategies. Finally they settled on a plan. "We had better disguise our classroom to look like the Fortress of Fear by tomorrow morning," said Thekla.

"Agreed," said Sammy. He and Thekla shook hands.

"Historic moment," said Lois. "And won't Miss Earth be surprised to learn that she's getting her Christmas wish—the Tattletales and Copycats working together."

Reebok thumped his tail on the floor of the Grand Union and muttered out of the side of his mouth, "Can we go now? The smell of eighty sacks of dog food in aisle five is really getting to me."

✳

The meeting at Grandma Earth's went smooth as eggnog. All fifteen classmates were there, as well as Miss Earth and her mother. Since Reebok was Lois's dog, Lois stood up to speak first.

"Folks," Lois said, "what you are about to hear is cause for shock and amazement. But you must promise never to reveal what you now learn. Deal?"

"Deal," they all said.

"You're on," said Lois to Reebok.

The dog jumped up onto the rolling tool tray and said, "Please don't tell anyone else I can talk. As soon as I can afford to lose this little contraption, I will take a vow of silence. If I must make a remark, frankly, I prefer my native tongue. But this situation is too serious."

"But how can you talk?" said Miss Earth.

"Actually," Reebok began, "some aliens from the planet of Fixipuddle are visiting Earth and—"

"Miss Earth," interrupted Thekla Mustard, "if we want to save Mayor Grass, we have to be ready by eight o'clock tomorrow morning. We'll have to take it on faith that Reebok can talk, and move on from there."

"You see," Reebok continued, "the Fixipuddlings are wrong about a lot of things. They don't know what it means to be human. Neither do I, but at least I don't try to kidnap anyone to find out. The Fixipuddlings don't know how to have fun. They don't know about stories. The Fixipuddlings think that the dolls and tin soldiers and teddy bears you get for presents are all *spies* for Santa."

Lois Kennedy the Third tightened her belt around her spy coat and pulled her snap-brimmed hat down over her eyebrows. They wanted spies? She could show them *spies*.

Sammy Grubb took up the story. "Thekla

Mustard and I have guessed that the only way we can convince the Fixipuddlings that they've actually liberated the planet is if we construct a Fortress of Fear in our classroom. We will have to pretend to be elves disguised as human children. And we'll have to sacrifice all our toys, I'm afraid, so that the toys can appear to be the next batch of Santa's spies. We have to pretend to be torturing them and training them to be vicious spies."

The children gasped when they realized what it was going to cost, not just in nerves but in long-awaited Christmas booty.

Grandma Earth and Miss Earth looked at each other. Miss Earth cleared her throat. "It's funny," she said. "Normally I would think this sounds like some plot out of *I Love Lucy*. But if we can get back our beloved mayor through this harebrained scheme—"

"Then I say," added Grandma Earth, because her daughter was getting all choked up, "let's go brain some hares!"

Miss Earth blew her nose. This time it wasn't the flu.

Once she had gotten her voice back, she took over like the excellent teacher she was. "Luckily it's a Friday night," she said. "I'll make some calls to your parents and tell them we're having an impromptu sleepover at the school. Then I'll call Jasper Stripe, the janitor, and have him come in and rev up the furnace. All you kids go home and collect your pajamas. Also bring any leftover candy canes, knee socks, ribbons and bows, and red and green sweaters. Also bring your Christmas presents, new or old, and don't forget your toothbrushes. Even during a local emergency, cavities are just waiting to happen in your mouths."

"My dad can send over some takeout curry from our restaurant, the Mango Tree," said Salim. "He'd be delighted. He loves to feed America."

"I'll bring my old treadle sewing machine in the pickup," said Grandma Earth. "I'll need it."

"If no one has a little leg of lamb to give me as a reward," shouted Reebok, "well then, on to other things. On your mark, get set, go." And off everybody ran.

*

In many schools it would be hard to organize a sleepover just like that. But Hamlet, Vermont, was a small town. All the parents knew Miss Earth personally. They trusted her and admired her. They thought perhaps she was being sensitive to the children's fears about the missing Mayor Grass. They thought she was trying to cheer the children up with a surprise treat. Every child received permission. "Have fun!" called the parents.

Fun? *Fun?* Hardly. It was a night of hard work and careful concentration. More than once, tears were spilt at the thought of parting with their beloved holiday toys.

Thekla and Sammy had decided on a fairly simple idea. What did the alien elves expect Santa's workshop to be like? A place where slave labor worked night and day making Santa's spies. The five Fixipuddlings didn't know what toys were. They didn't know that soldiers and dolls and teddy bears were for fun. They hadn't watched enough of that Christmas movie to see children waking up in the morning to shouts of surprise and delight.

So in order to convince the Fixipuddlings that Santa's work force was waiting to be liberated, the children had to look as if they were slaving at a factory. The loyal students and their teacher set out to re-create the Fortress of Fear in Miss Earth's room.

Grandma Earth sat at her sewing machine, doing up little felt hats for the boys and little white aprons for the girls.

Miss Earth rushed around the room, hiding evidence of teaching. Luckily the room was still decorated with pine boughs and colored lights from the holiday party on Christmas Eve.

The Copycats, the Tattletales, and Pearl Hotchkiss stood at their work tables, creating little dioramas of pain out of their presents. They were sacrificing their favorite toys to the cause! "This really *is* the Ghost of Christmas Presents," said Fawn Petros, and for once nobody could argue with her.

At one table was a huge pile of teddy bears from Christmases way back when the kids were young. Hector Yellow and Pearl Hotchkiss sat there with scissors, snipping off their kindly button eyes. In their place Hector and Pearl sewed squinty dots, with inward-slanting eyebrows to make the bears scowl. (Hector had brought his dad's electric razor, and he wanted to give all the bears thuggish haircuts, but he was voted down on that one.)

Mike Saint Michael, Stan Tomaski, and Nina Bueno had about thirty Barbie dolls to work with. They had Jump Rope Barbie, Cheerleader Barbie, Prom Barbie, Bridal Barbie. They had Doctor Barbie, Lawyer Barbie, and Indian Chief Barbie. They had Butcher Barbie, Baker Barbie, and Candlestick Maker Barbie. They had Eenie Barbie, Meanie Barbie, Miney Barbie, and Mohawk Barbie. They even had Mata Hari Barbie, who came dressed in a trench coat and a man's fedora. She looked a lot like Lois Kennedy the Third, except without the red plastic boots.

All the Barbies had their heads cut off with a hacksaw. The heads were glued to the tops of Christmas cookies on a cookie tray. Sharday Wren and Moshe Cohn brought the Playmate plastic stove from Ms. Frazzle's kindergarten classroom, and they made a sign to hang above it. It read THE BRAINWASHING CHAMBER.

The baby dolls were too cute to do anything very nasty with, but Fawn Petros and Carly Garfunkel took an especially gooey-eyed baby doll and tied her with jump ropes to the train tracks that Hector Yellow had gotten for Christmas. It was clear that an electric train running into a big baby would derail itself with horrible consequences to its passengers. It wouldn't do the baby much good, either. Fawn and Carly put some old-fashioned plastic cowboys and Indians on the roof of the train, so you could imagine how far they'd fly once they hit the big baby.

Salim Bannerjee hadn't gotten any Christmas or Hanukkah presents, so he had nothing to contribute. But he spent the night writing spy lessons on the blackboard in colored chalk.

SPIES: REMEMBER!
TELL SANTA EVERYTHING YOU SEE *OR ELSE!*
BACK TO THE FORTRESS OF FEAR FOR MORE *TORTURE!*

Anna Maria Mastrangelo had received her first-ever nail polish for Christmas. Though it was called Sicilian Rose, anyone could tell it was really Dried Blood. Anna Maria wandered around the room with it, adding a little touch here and there. "Impressive," she said, "ya gotta admit it."

When they were done, Miss Earth told the kids to settle down. But they were all too antsy. So she decided a little healthful exercise outside, stretching their large muscle groups, might tire them out. Miss Earth chose Pearl Hotchkiss, Sammy Grubb, and Thekla Mustard to direct three bands of children. Each group got busy rolling a boulder of snow. When there were three massive pieces, all the kids got together and heaved one on top of the other.

It was nine feet tall. It was beautiful. The kids packed more snow in the chinks. It began to look more like a concrete cone than anything else. When it was too tall for them to reach any higher, even with one kid standing on the shoulders of another, they gathered pine branches from the edge of the playground. Carefully they shredded long pine needles off the boughs and stuck the pine needles in the snowman. It took forever, but little by little the snowman began to look like a creature with greenish-brownish hair. They used two cookies for eyes.

"It looks like Pimplemuss," said Reebok. Then he crawled under Miss Earth's desk and slept the night away. The children hoped he might talk in his sleep, and he did, but all he said was "Rabbit!" and then "Squirrel!" and then "Chateaubriand with a little green peppercorn glaze?"

Pearl ate a doughnut and then went to brush her teeth. Sammy was standing at the classroom sink, brushing his teeth, too. "Aren't you a little embarrassed that what you heard in the woods wasn't Bigfoot?" said Pearl in a low voice. Sammy only pointed to his mouth, full of toothpaste suds. But he turned red and didn't answer her even when his mouth was empty. He went over to the bookshelf and found a paperback copy of *The Wizard of Oz* and began to read it.

At last the classmates slept, waking when the sun began to rise, a pale papery orange above coal black hills. The children got into their costumes and ate the doughnuts that Grandma Earth had brought from her bakery. Then they sat down to await the invasion of the alien elves.

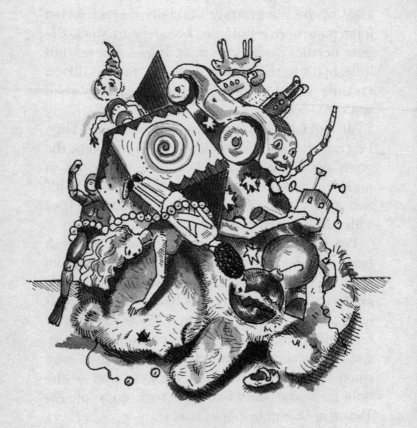

20

Bigfoot, Pimplemuss, and the Ghost of Christmas Presents

Reebok woke up and poked the air with his nose. "Get ready," he said. "They're coming."

Miss Earth opened the classroom door that led to the snow-trampled playground. The cold air came in and made everyone feel more awake. She said, "Places, everyone. And do be on your best behavior. Whatever happens, you have given me my Christmas wish: Boys and girls, you have all worked together admirably. For that, thank you. Now, you should try to look careworn and over-worked. But that won't be hard, given that you *are* careworn and overworked."

Grandma Earth was hunched over her sewing machine. Miss Earth got down on her hands and knees with a bucket of sudsy water she'd drawn from Jasper Stripe's sink. The children all took up their stations at their work desks.

Reebok stuck his head out the open door. He began to yap with convincing panic. "Friends! Here! Over here!" he called.

Lois Kennedy the Third had been chosen to do the honors. She was pretending to be the head spy. She wore her spy outfit and prowled up and down between the desks, lecturing the toys on how to snoop for Santa Claus. "Toys! Listen up! You must see the Earthlings when they're sleeping! You should know when they're awake!" she cried. "You must report back if they've been bad or good! And you better do it, or that'll be a big mistake! And if I see you so much as twitch a plastic eyebrow, I'll have your heads—again!"

She strode with a stiff gait to the classroom door that opened out into the schoolyard. She glanced out and said in a carrying voice, "Oh, look. Some more elves to help us at our backbreaking labor. Won't you come in?" (She'd been practicing that line all night.)

Reebok had described the alien elves so well that all the children knew exactly who was who. Pimplemuss led the way, an old dwarf with a face like an apple that had fallen out of the basket and spent the season unnoticed behind some boots in the mud room.

"So, we meet at last," said Pimplemuss. She didn't recognize Lois from before, because Lois had not been wearing her spy outfit the last time. "If Reebok has showed up already, then you must

142

know why we're here. We have come to liberate you from your drudgery."

"You're welcome here," said Lois grandly. "Come in and tell us more."

The young ones followed Pimplemuss. Droyd and Peppa were holding hands. They were only about as big as Lois's baby brother, maybe two feet tall. They had rosy cheeks and dimples and Droyd was missing a tooth. It made him look like a kid in a commercial for breakfast cereal.

Foomie was next. Foomie's hair had been decorated with little ribbons and bows, but still fell all around Foomie's head like dying chives drooping out of a pot.

The fierce old Pimplemuss must have relented, once Reebok had escaped, and changed Narr back from a pile of dog food. For there was Narr, bringing up the rear. Narr was fingering his beard, which was wriggling as if it wanted to get away and be someplace else.

"Where did you run off to?" said Pimplemuss to Reebok. "You caused us no end of worry."

"Sorry," said Reebok. "I got lost in the woods and only found my way back here this morning. I had a little breakfast with my friends here at the Fortress of Fear. I was just about to come look for you. Really I was."

Droyd and Peppa wandered around the classroom looking at the grisly displays. "Oh, that awful Santa Claws!" said Foomie, following them. "Look at the terrible things he makes them do to these agents as he prepares to sneak them into people's houses! Santa Claws tortures them until they agree to spy on the Earthlings!"

"I had no choice," said Lois. "There would be no end of trouble from that dictator if I refused his orders."

"Elves of the world, unite!" cried Pimplemuss. "You have nothing to lose but your chains! You can also lose those ugly disguises as human children you seem to be reconditioned into."

"What do you mean?" said Miss Earth, looking up from her scrub brush and rubbing a wet hand across her pretty brow.

"I mean that Santa Claws has been captured! His reign of terror on Earth is over! You can stop this awful work of torturing and brainwashing these fabricated creatures! You are free to rise and throw off your shackles!"

This was the part that required the best acting. The children had to:

- look unbelieving (open their eyes wide)
- act frightened (nibble their fingernails and clutch each other)
- slowly turn from timid to brave (bit lips turn into small smiles)
- shout and cheer and jump up and down (a lot)

But Miss Earth's class was up to the challenge. Each and every one of them was a ham at heart.

The only one who felt shy at first was Salim Bannerjee. He was not only new to the school but still new to the American way of life. But since life in Bombay had supplied him his own kind of South Asian chutzpah, he fit right in.

The children's shouting and cheering and jumping up and down were certainly convincing. Some of the kids found themselves acting so well that they almost convinced themselves that their years of bondage to an evil dictator were really at an end! (Lois managed this by substituting the idea of Thekla Mustard for the idea of Santa Claus.) Several eyes got teary. Several noses were blown. Several kids overdid this part, but fortunately by then even the alien elves were weeping. Pimplemuss climbed up on the sewing machine and threw her arms around Grandma Earth. Narr dabbed his eyes with his beard. Foomie tried to blow Foomie's nose but couldn't even find it underneath all that hair.

Droyd and Peppa wandered around looking at the toys. Droyd wanted to set the electric train running and make it crash into the giant baby tied to the tracks. Peppa slapped his hand and said, "It's all behind them now, Droyd. Let it go. Let it all go."

When the children had just about run through their repertoire of expressions of joy, Miss Earth said, "And what about this Santa Claus, our former evil boss and tyrant? Now that we are freed, surely you will release him to join us? We will teach him to be nice instead of nasty."

"That's what we had intended," said Pimplemuss, beaming broadly, "but we've changed our minds. We're going to take him back to Fixipuddle with us."

"To where?" said Miss Earth. She straightened up.

"To our home planet. We've decided we want to open our own Fixipuddle Museum of Interesting Facts to Know and Tell. He can be the first exhibit."

"But why? Why?"

Pimplemuss beamed. "He's been telling us a strange and novel history of this perplexed man named Ebenezer Scrooge. It's fascinating. We think everyone in Fixipuddle would want to hear about him. And there's this sad, sickly child-thing named Tiny Tim who needs love and kindness. So we'll bring Santa Claws with us to tell everyone about what happens to poor Tiny Tim and the miserable Scrooge."

Miss Earth pulled herself to her feet. "But you can't!" she cried. She came forward in a pleading way. "You mustn't!"

"I smell a rat!" said Pimplemuss. She clenched her fists and advanced on Miss Earth. "Why do you want him back? You can't possibly be an oppressed enslaved elf if you want him back!"

Miss Earth blushed.

"I remember you! You're that creature they all thought was so beautiful!" cried Pimplemuss.

"Oh, pshaw," said Miss Earth. "Beauty is only skin deep. As you should know, being so good-hearted as to free us from our slavery."

"Are you implying that I am *ugly?*" cried Pimplemuss. "My beauty is more than skin deep!"

"Well, I don't want to quibble over measurements," stammered Miss Earth.

Pimplemuss's little old face began to turn orange and blue.

"Oh, no," said Droyd and Peppa. "Pimplemuss, don't!"

"My beauty is *all the way through!*" roared the leader of the Fixipuddlings.

"I'm sure it's quite deep, as far as it goes," said Miss Earth, nodding and gabbling.

"I'm a darn sight prettier than you are, you skinny clump of celery!" bellowed Pimplemuss. And at that the old woman elf disappeared in a scattering of orange and blue sparks. In her place stood the Fixipuddling commander of the starship *Loiterbug.*

She was marvelous and terrible to behold. She was nine feet tall, with a head that tapered into nothing but a beak and some earshells. Her six eyes were bloodshot with rage, one underneath the other. Her three legs and feet were shaggy like a white bear's, and her whole body was covered with white feathers of some sort.

"She looks like a mutant cousin of Big Bird on *Sesame Street,*" muttered Thekla Mustard.

"The original Bigfoot!" cried Sammy Grubb.

Pimplemuss looked at one of her three feet. "A big foot is a sign of beauty in a Fixipuddling!" she told them. "All right, you sneaky things, who's the most beautiful one of all *now*? Hmmmmm?"

She advanced on Miss Earth. The children were in a turmoil. What should they do? Miss Earth always believed in peace and harmony! Were they to attack this visitor from another planet?

It was quite a pickle.

But before they could decide, Reebok barked out, "Look! It's the *real Bigfoot*!" And he grabbed the string of the Venetian blinds in his mouth and backed up. As he went, the blinds were raised.

Outside the window was the nine-foot-tall snow monster. The children had capped the creature with the Santa Claus hat that Lois had found in Foggy Hollow.

Pimplemuss cried, "Everyone stand back! I'll save you!"

She ran out the door, bonking her beak on the top of the frame as she went. She flung herself on the snow monster and knocked it over.

"Oh my gracious," said Peppa, "its eyes came off!"

"It's shedding!" said Droyd.

Narr ate the end of his beard and began to choke.

Pimplemuss rolled and wrestled with the snowy Bigfoot until at last she opened her mouth and roared her triumph. What she didn't realize was that the internal body temperatures of Fixi-puddlings are a good deal warmer than those of snow monsters. So she was surprised when Bigfoot started to steam and hiss.

"It's melting," said Pearl. She couldn't help but add, "Oh, what a world, what a world." Soon there was little left but the Santa hat, three charred pine cones, and a puddle of water.

"There," said Pimplemuss, "I've rescued your planet twice. Now I'll surely be elected Serene Queen of Fixipuddling!"

21

The Queen of the Planet

Pimplemuss picked herself up and fluffed up her feathers. "Another victory against tyranny and fear!" she said. She swaggered a little as she came back into the classroom.

Lois Kennedy the Third had a brainstorm. She tossed her snap-brimmed hat in the air. "Oh, Pimplemuss!" she cried. "You've rescued us from an even worse enemy! Bigfoot the Snow Monster! Hail to the Fixipuddlings, saviors of our species!"

"Hail," said Grandma Earth uneasily. She didn't like to give homage to anyone.

"Hail," said Miss Earth, who tended to agree with her mother. "Hail, indeed." She lowered her eyes and used an end bristle on her scrub brush to poke underneath her fingernail. "Hail and farewell," she muttered.

But the children understood. They were all revved up from their earlier act. "Oh, hail to the Fixipuddlings! Yayyyyy!"

"Hip hip," growled Reebok, "hooray."

"Speech!" cried Thekla.

"Speech, speech!" the others chorused.

You could tell Pimplemuss was pleased. Droyd and Peppa rushed up to her and stood smiling on either side, like the children of a candidate for president. Narr and Foomie looked suspicious at first—was this a trick? But when nothing bad happened, they relaxed.

Pimplemuss was persuaded to make a few remarks. "Dear Earthlings," she said, "today a dream has come true. Many years ago when I was but a little Pimplekitten, I accidentally exploded a planet in our home galaxy—"

"You *did*?" cried Droyd and Peppa in disbelief.

"It was an accident, as I say," Pimplemuss hurried on.

"But how could you wreck a *planet*?" asked Sammy Grubb, in awe and respect.

"No need to go into specifics," said Pimplemuss. "I probably needed a little Time Out. Never mind about all that. Luckily nobody was on the planet at the time. Everyone had gone on vacation to another galaxy. Well, I would have liked to remake that planet I wrecked. But of course that's impossible. So I resolved to become Serene Queen of Fixipuddle. Think of the noble things I could do as Serene Queen! But to be eligible I had to liberate a planet from dictatorship. This I have done. So now I can leave you all and go home and do some good."

"You can do some good right now. Release your prisoner," said Grandma Earth.

"Oh, no," said Pimplemuss. "I am going to do ever so much more good than I had originally planned. I am going to do googolplexes of good. I am going to bring Santa Claws back to Fixipuddle. Because he tells such a strange . . . what's that word . . . a story! We think that the Fixipuddlings back home would love to hear it. And maybe he knows more."

"But he can't go," said Miss Earth.

"*Says—who?*" said Pimplemuss in that gonglike tone of voice she had. Narr and Foomie looked worried.

"We all say so," said Miss Earth. She put down her scrub brush. She straightened her spine. The children knew that look. It meant: The time for fun and games was over.

"Now, Pimplemuss," said Miss Earth, "here's what you must do. You must lead us back to your starship and return Mayor Timothy Grass to our midst. We are all tired and we've had about enough."

"And who are you to be taking such a high and mighty tone with Pimplemuss of Fixipuddle?" roared the alien.

"I," said Miss Earth, "am Miss Earth."

Pimplemuss blinked her eyes, one after the other. "This is the *planet* Earth and you are called *Miss* Earth?" she said slowly.

"As it happens, yes," said Miss Earth. She took off her white apron and folded it up on her desk.

"And so do *you* run the dread Fortress of Fear?" said Pimplemuss.

"You're quite mistaken about the Fortress of Fear," said Miss Earth.

The children all held their breath. Was their teacher going to give it all away?

Yes, she was.

"Adults can make mistakes as well as children and visitors from outer space," said Miss Earth firmly. "In my concern for Mayor Grass's safety, I allowed myself to be carried away from my principles. I entered into a little white lie. But in fact I don't believe in fibbing, even of the gentle sort. I made a mistake. I should not have endorsed the idea of our pretending to run the Fortress of Fear. It goes against the grain. Pimplemuss, there is no such thing. You have misunderstood."

"There must be a Fortress of Fear!" said Pimplemuss. "Otherwise, what's to liberate?"

Miss Earth answered, "You have to liberate yourself from a wrong idea."

Pimplemuss looked wary. Her lower lip shot out and wobbled.

"You are old enough to know better. This is not appropriate behavior when you visit a new planet. Stand up straight when I speak to you."

The children were aghast. Miss Earth *never* talked teacherish.

153

"Just because you blew up a planet sometime in your silly youth is no reason to go traipsing around the galaxy causing trouble for other folks. You are scared that no one will like you unless you save them, but that's not true. The only Fortress of Fear is in your heart. You have locked yourself up in there. But you can give up on this silly campaign. You can accept the fact that your friends and relations love you as you are. You don't need to earn merit badges or win elections."

Pimplemuss began to sniffle. "Nobody could love me, really!"

"That's not true," said Peppa and Droyd. "We love you, Pimplemuss."

Narr nodded his head, vigorously.

"Well," admitted Foomie, "it's true I've become *attached* to you, in a weird sort of way."

"In the spirit of the season," said Miss Earth, "I ask you to let Mayor Grass go."

Pimplemuss sniffed. "I thought we understood the spirit of the season."

"We will tell you the stories of the Christmas season if you like," said Miss Earth. "They're all about peace on Earth, good will to all people, but I suppose they can also be about peace in outer space and good will to all creatures everywhere, even Fixipuddlings."

She picked up the book on her desk, and turned to the last page. She read, "'Scrooge was better than his word. He did it all, and infinitely more;

and to Tiny Tim, who did *not* die, he was a second father. He became as good a friend, as good a master, and as good a man, as the good old city knew, or any other good old city, town, or borough, in the good old world.'" Miss Earth paused and improved on Dickens by adding, "Including good old planets out there somewhere."

She continued another few lines, and ended, "'It was always said of him, that he knew how to keep Christmas well, if any man alive possessed the knowledge. May that be truly said of us, and all of us! And so, as Tiny Tim observed, God Bless Us, Every One!'"

Droyd and Peppa were in cascades of joyous tears. So was Salim. Even salty old Grandma Earth had to hide her face in her apron.

"God Bless Us, *Every* One," intoned Miss Earth, a little more gently.

"Miss Earth," said Pimplemuss, and then she couldn't speak anymore. She was sobbing with gratitude and new understanding. There wasn't enough Kleenex in the box to take care of the flood, so Miss Earth just handed over her apron.

"There, there," said Miss Earth, coming up to Pimplemuss and putting her arms as far around the Fixipuddling as they would reach. "It's all right. That's a good alien."

"And now we'd better go get Tim from your starship," said Grandma Earth.

Miss Earth added, "Mayor Tim Grass is not

exactly poor little Tiny Tim, but he still needs a better Christmas than the one he got."

"You said it, sweetheart! How about a little beef stew to celebrate?" said Reebok. Everyone looked at him. "I'm merely asking," he said.

All the children put on their outside clothes and followed the aliens back to the starship. Several cars drove by, and people waved and smiled at Miss Earth, her mother, her students, and the giant white duck-bear thing. What a good teacher! They wondered who it could be in that costume, though. Usually it was good-natured Mayor Timothy Grass who ended up trudging around in that kind of getup. Oh where, oh where was Mayor Grass?

*

When they got to Old Man Fingerpie's barn, Pimplemuss turned to Miss Earth. "You truly are the Queen of the Planet," she said. "What I overheard your little elves say to you is true. You *could* be Miss Ultimate Reality in the Space-Time Continuum."

"Thank you," said Miss Earth. "But being a teacher is all I really want in life."

"Just one thing," said Pimplemuss. "I'm still confused. If there is no Fortress of Fear, then where does Santa Claws control his evil empire from?"

"You've got the idea of Santa Claus all wrong," said Miss Earth. "He's not a villain. He brings presents to little children. What you thought were industrial products made for spying and terror are actually *toys*. For fun. Little ones need to play in order to learn how to be grown up, but also in order to have *fun*."

"We agree with *that*," said Droyd.

"We never have *any* fun," said Peppa.

"Perhaps we could import the idea of *toys* to Fixipuddle!" said Pimplemuss.

Miss Earth went on. "Santa Claus brings joy and happiness to all. The way you would like to. The way you will. Santa is based on an older word meaning 'good' or 'holy.' Santa Claus isn't really a person anymore, it's an idea. An idea of generosity and kindness. It's the real Spirit of Christmas Past, Present, and Future. The word *Santa* is just a title, like Miss or Mayor or Grandma."

"Like Santa Pimplemuss?" said Pimplemuss.

"Perhaps," said Miss Earth.

"Santa Pimplemuss," said Pimplemuss. "Maybe I could earn a merit badge if I go back to Fixipuddle and start the toy tradition there. Maybe I don't need to be Serene Queen of Fixipuddle."

"Good idea," said Lois Kennedy the Third. She marched up to the alien and handed over the Santa Claus hat. It was the only salvageable thing left from the Bigfoot meltdown. "Santa Pimplemuss."

Pimplemuss put it on top of her nine-foot-high head. "Ho ho ho," she said, a little shyly. "How do I look?"

"You look wonderful," said Droyd and Peppa. Narr nodded.

"How do I know what you look like?" said Foomie. "I haven't seen a thing since you turned me into this hair disaster."

22

Up in the Sky
There Arose Such a Clatter

Mayor Grass couldn't believe his eyes. Into the starship *Loiterbug* came Pimplemuss and the other Fixipuddlings . . . and Miss Earth.

Impossible! How beautiful she looked! But was this *really* Miss Earth? Perhaps this was Reebok, changed by the particle shower to look like Miss Earth!

"We've arranged for your release, Tim," said Miss Earth, reaching behind his chair and loosening his bonds. She smelled heavenly, a blend of lavender bath splash and jelly doughnuts. It had to be her.

"My muscles are so stiff," he said.

Grandma Earth came in next. "Here, I have some Numb-All in my overalls pocket," she said. "It's great for stiff muscles. Can we get a glass of water here?" Narr hurried to obey.

The children wanted to come in the starship,

too. "I don't know if there's room," murmured Foomie, but kids make room when they want to. They clambered in, one after the other. All the kids had to crowd into the particle shower and make funny noises as if they were being zapped. They begged Pimplemuss to change them into something, but she wouldn't.

"Now that I know what a toy is, I can say emphatically, the particle shower is *not a toy*," she remarked sternly, sounding like a parent. Droyd and Peppa rolled their eyes.

When Mayor Grass stood up, he turned to Pimplemuss. She looked ashamed. "I suppose apologies are in order," she said. "I'm not going to take you away from your friends. They love you enough to stand up to aliens to protect you. It would be unkind of us to keep you all to ourselves. Though you do know some great stories!"

"Well," said Mayor Grass. He didn't feel like forgiving them just like that. "I was mighty uncomfortable."

"The thing is, I'm embarrassed by what happened," Pimplemuss continued. "I got carried away."

"I was afraid that *I* was about to get carried away," said Mayor Grass. "To another galaxy. But I suppose it wasn't your fault. You just picked up a Christmas movie on your video screen. Since you didn't know what stories are, you thought it was true."

"Well, you wouldn't have been carried away anytime soon," said Pimplemuss, "because after we had finished liberating the planet from the evil dictator, we'd have to worry about fixing the engine on this thing."

"What's your problem, lady?" said Grandma Earth, rolling up her shirtsleeves.

"It's the fibrillator fins, we think. They got choked and something burned out," said Pimplemuss.

Grandma Earth pulled a section of the floor up and peered into the engine below. "Anyone got a flashlight?" she said. Foomie found one and handed it to her. "Hmmm. Interesting. Reminds me of a 1924 Hupmobile. Guard my back, Germaine," she said to her daughter. "I'm going down." And she climbed down a ladder into the engine.

"I'm hungry," said Mayor Grass. "Do you think you could transform some more of those sea slugs into something like ham and eggs?"

"I shall never do harm to another living creature," said Pimplemuss. "The sea slugs shall go free!" She clomped into the galley and drew up a ladleful of grinning sea slugs, who had heard her pronouncement and were slapping one another's tiny hands in a high-five sign.

"Not on our planet, please," said Miss Earth. "They may have no natural predators. If they repopulate themselves, they could take over the world."

The sea slugs liked this idea. They all nodded vigorously.

"I see your point," said Pimplemuss, and dropped the sea slugs back in the keg. "I'll release them back home in the Saucy Sea of Fixipuddle."

"Wrench," bawled Grandma Earth. "Tweezers. Pipe cleaner. What a mess! Don't you ever change your spark plugs? Your oil's good, though. You can go another sixty, eighty billion miles without having to worry, I think. Screwdriver."

Narr and Foomie rushed around finding the right tools. Within a few minutes, Grandma said, "Well, that's a wrap, I think." She emerged from the floor below, oil smudges on her cheeks and forehead.

"Shall I fire her up?" said Foomie.

"We can take you for a little ride and then drop you off at the Fortress of Fear—I mean at the Josiah Fawcett Elementary School," said Pimplemuss.

"Some people think that schools are always Fortresses of Fear," said Miss Earth.

"Not *us*," cried her students. "Ours is a Fortress of *Fun*!"

Their teacher corrected them. "Fun, but also learning and good manners. What do you say about that kind idea?"

"Yes, please, Santa Pimplemuss," they chorused.

"Fire up the back burners." cried Pimplemuss. "We're off to Fixipuddle, with a detour on the way!"

The children crowded to the windows. There was a smell of motor oil and the sound of pumping pistons. In a very short while, the starship *Loiterbug* was lifting slowly, heavily, away from the ground.

But how heavenly to fly! The kids could see the roof of Old Man Fingerpie's barn. As the starship passed it, more snow flew off the roof. Owls scattered from the eaves. The dark asphalt roofing became smaller, a rectangle of gray in all the snow around. There was Squished Toad Road, there was Bumpy Road, there was Hardscrabble Road, there was Ethan Allen Park. And everywhere, on all sides, the hills and trees that make Vermont so beautiful.

"There *is* no place like home," said Miss Earth happily.

"I still think it's kind of ugly," mumbled Droyd to Peppa. Peppa poked him to make him shut up.

Far too quickly, the starship *Loiterbug* settled down in the schoolyard. It melted the snow beneath it and scorched the dead grass in a cryptic shape, which reporters came from all over the country to photograph. The following week it would be on the cover of the *National Town Crier,* with the headline WINTER SLUGS CHEW MYSTERY MESSAGE TO THE PLANET!

But today, Grandma Earth and Miss Earth helped Mayor Grass get out. All the schoolchildren jumped down by themselves. "We're not going to stay," cried Pimplemuss through the open hatchway. The other Fixipuddlings stood around her, waving. "We've got to get back to our own planet and start our new tradition of holiday cheer!"

"Just one moment, though," called Miss Earth.

She huddled with her students. They all nodded at her suggestion, and then they ran through the door to their classroom. They were back a minute later.

"Christmas presents," said Miss Earth. "More or less."

"On behalf of the students of Miss Earth's class," said Lois Kennedy the Third, "we would like to make our first contribution to the notion of Toys in Space."

Each child had an armload of wrecked dolls, bears, and soldiers. "You can have fun putting them back together," said Lois.

"Cool," said Peppa, leaning out of the hatchway.

"Neat," said Droyd, right beside her.

"Thanks," they said together.

"Fun," murmured Pimplemuss. "It'll take a while for me to understand it."

"Another thing," said Miss Earth. "I thought Droyd and Peppa might like these."

Droyd and Peppa reached down their hands. Miss Earth had a box of gold stars with glue on the back. "For good behavior," she said. "Because it's a long trip home."

"Thank you, Miss Earth," they said.

"And for you," said Miss Earth to Pimplemuss. She handed over a paperback from her shelf of favorites. "It's a book."

"Does it bleep or have interactive noises or lights?"

"Not exactly," said Miss Earth. "But it is packed

with story from beginning to end. It will tell you a little bit about how to be human. Then if you ever come back for a visit, you'll still be a Fixipuddling but you won't be an alien. All *alien* means is 'foreigner,' and if you know the stories of human beings, you're not foreign anymore."

Pimplemuss blinked her six eyes to hold back tears.

"Wow," said Pearl Hotchkiss, looking at the spine. "It's *The Wizard of Oz.* It's about this girl who goes to another planet, kind of, and meets these weird creatures—"

"Don't tell us! We want to read it ourselves!" cried Foomie. "Though I can't imagine any weirder creatures than you, not to put too fine a point on it."

"One more present," cried Lois Kennedy the Third. She raced back into the classroom and came out again. In her arms were the fifteen Christmas stockings that had been hung on the bulletin board with care. She handed them up to the aliens in the hatchway. "You can use these to keep all your feet warm! There's fifteen socks and five of you, three feet each once Droyd and Peppa grow up—what could be better?"

"How thoughtful," said Pimplemuss. "Our feet are always cold, especially in this snowy wasteland. And paper socks have never really satisfied. Thank you."

"Come and visit us again, please," said Miss

Earth. "Next time you're in the neighborhood."
She began to sing in her tuneless way, "We wish you
a Merry Christmas . . ."

Reebok sang solo on the line, "Now bring us a
figgy pudding . . ."

"Oh," said Pimplemuss, and looked sternly at
Droyd and Peppa. "It's a figgy pudding they wanted,
not a Fixipuddling."

"Shoot. I could have made you a real figgy pudding to take home with you as a souvenir," said
Grandma Earth. "The first intergalactic holiday
fruitcake. Oh, well. If you're ever this way again,
don't hesitate to stop by and I'll whip one up for
you in a flash."

Reebok was inspired to invent some new verses.
He sang, "So bring me a whole lasagna, then bring
me a quarter-pounder, then bring me a roast of sirloin, and bring it right now. Then bring me a side
of French fries, then bring me a side of coleslaw,
then bring—"

Despite his stiff limbs, Mayor Timothy Grass
leaned down and unbuckled the WordSearch dial.
He tossed it to Narr. Reebok kept howling, tune-
lessly, in a fierce appetite for food, or maybe for
fine holiday music.

The starship *Loiterbug* lifted off as the children
took up the song again. It shimmied and shivered
as they sang, and then it flew out of sight.

*

Anyone who happened to be tuned in to WAAK, the Voice of Vermont, heard Ernie Latucci say, "You know, folks, I was just walking back from the men's room when I looked out the window and saw a bright light streak across the sky! It was like nothing I ever saw before! UFOs in the USA? Call 1-800-555-WAAK and tell us about your experiences being abducted by space aliens!"

But he didn't get any calls from Mayor Timothy Grass.

✳

After the New Year, Lois Kennedy the Third proposed an election for Empress of the Tattletales. "Why?" said Thekla Mustard.

"Because you always get to be Empress," said Lois.

"So?"

"I was the one who discovered the Fixipuddlings."

"No, you didn't. Reebok did."

"Well, Reebok is *my* dog."

"He talked too much. And he was so *greedy*."

"Thekla, I demand a vote. It isn't fair for you to be Empress all the time."

"Democracy is always fair," said Thekla. "Still, if the girls want you to be Empress, fine with me. I shall retire and write my memoirs."

The election went in Thekla's favor. Five votes for Thekla, two for Lois. Lois voted for herself, but Fawn Petros voted for her, too. It was the first time

Lois had ever gotten another vote, so she considered that she had made some progress. Lois contented herself by remembering that sometimes you don't get elected to your role in life. You just choose it. After all, who had elected Santa Claus? Nobody. He just made himself up. And Santa Pimplemuss was making herself up too.

Not that she wanted to be Santa Lois Kennedy the Third. But she could think about it. Something would occur to her.

Besides, Mayor Tim Grass—who never admitted to a soul where he had been for almost a week, because who would believe him?—took Lois aside one day and said, "You know, it was your dog Reebok who really set things up for my release. It was Reebok who figured out how to get Pimplemuss to Miss Earth's class. And then Pimplemuss succumbed to Miss Earth's common sense. Reebok might be awfully hungry, but he put his own appetites second to securing my release. So in a way I have you to thank, for raising such a good dog."

"You're welcome," said Lois. "Does this mean I don't have to pay for a dog license next year?"

"No," said the mayor. "That would be wrong. You have to pay like everyone else. But Reebok can wear his dog tag with special pride. I'll borrow a gold star from Miss Earth to put on it myself."

✳

Mayor Timothy Grass finished reading *Helpless in Hollywood*. At the end, the president asked Spangles O'Leary to marry him. This gave Mayor Grass an idea. Maybe he'd loan *Helpless in Hollywood* to Miss Earth. Maybe she'd like it as much as he did. Maybe she would see they had some things in common, like the enjoyment of literary masterpieces. It might make her like him better. It was worth a try.

✳

On New Year's Eve, Sammy Grubb was walking home through Foggy Hollow and realized: Just because Pimplemuss wasn't Bigfoot didn't mean that Bigfoot wasn't still out there somewhere.

That was the great thing about New Year's Eve: A whole year was waiting right next door to this one, just about to start. A new year during which creatures like Bigfoot might invade the town and terrorize its people! It just made you glad to be alive.

✳

Pearl Hotchkiss thought about it some more. Pimplemuss had looked a little bit like Bigfoot—or at least a kind of Bigfowl. So Sammy Grubb hadn't been all that far off. Pearl felt she could go back to admiring Sammy Grubb again. He was so besotted with hunting for Bigfoot that he didn't notice. Which was just fine with her. For now.

169

Halfway back to the planet of Fixipuddle, Foomie was still at work repairing the broken scan-o-matic. Narr was driving the starship *Loiterbug*. Droyd and Peppa, playing with the toys, started singing again. Foomie joined in. Narr grinned worriedly and kept time by tapping one of his three feet.

Pimplemuss came from her chamber carrying a cup of corn tea. She was wearing her new sleeping socks—three Christmas stockings, red and green wool with reindeer patterns. She said crossly, "Will you stop singing that *song*? You're driving me crazy!"

"We're not singing to you," said Foomie. "We're singing to the starship *Loiterbug*. It's kind of catchy, isn't it?" Even the liberated sea slugs swayed back and forth and clapped their tiny hands in rhythm.

"So bring us to Fixipuddle, so bring us to Fixipuddle,
So bring us to Fixipuddle, and bring us right now!"

It was going to be a long trip, but they could sing for a few hundred light years. The new stockings would keep them warm. They were well into their new story, and enjoying it a lot. Having fun.

Outside and all around, the stars and planets twinkled like universal Christmas lights.